MADISON MURPHY

JESSICA GLEASON

Published by Cupid's Arrow Publishing
cupidsarrowpublishing.com

ISBN 978-1-967547-75-3 (Trade Paperback)

10 9 8 7 6 5 4 3 2 1

Madison is a testament to my youth, 23, at teaching college English while still a child myself. So, to younger me, thank you for taking the time to write this book.

Thank you to everyone who helped me along the way, Rebecca Hogan, Jeanine Fassl, and Alison Townsend. Without your guidance I may never have nourished my talents. You all changed my life in ways I may never fully comprehend.

MADISON MURPHY

1

I T'S OFFICIAL.

Madison Murphy unknowingly kissed her lackadaisical Wisconsin lifestyle goodbye. She'd lost her laid-back privileges somewhere between banging her blind date and waking up naked on the living room floor next to a stack of uncooked meat. Confused and terrified, she shuddered on the less than clean floor of her home, a pool of meat juices seeping into her wooden floors and a large pile of what looked like cat puke drying near her head. Confused and ashamed, Madison didn't understand her odd situation. But, after a day of heaving hairballs, she began to connect the dots. Her terrible date had infected her with some unfortunate affliction. She was too embarrassed to see a doctor, but noticed her appetite, temper, and appearance had changed.

Madison always struggled with her body. Even when she was skinny by Western standards, she'd look in the mirror to see an overweight weirdo. Over time she'd gained weight and her body image only worsened. She developed an off-putting self-deprecating sense of humor to shield herself from the world. It didn't matter if she lost a few pounds or wore a flattering dress, she only saw a pudgy monster. Since her unfortunate blind date, her body image had taken a nose dive right off a cliff. She'd gained the ability to change into a stupid Siberian tiger at a moment's notice—as if that was a useful skill. Maybe a fire-breathing dragon or a cute little pixie fairy ...

But a Siberian tiger?

Not so much, especially in Wisconsin.

Tigers aren't exactly running around in the wild in the Midwestern United States. Perhaps if she'd woken up as a deer she could have fit in. Though, her chances of getting an arrow through the gullet would have probably risen tenfold.

Madison had always felt othered, out of place. The ability to turn into a gigantic kitty cat every time she got upset certainly didn't help her learn to love herself or teach her to fit in. She'd taken a while to come to terms with her situation and instead of embracing a phenomenal new ability, she hated it with a fiery passion. One body was tough for her; two felt impossible.

Her temper flared as she realized she could never leave the house again. Maybe were she a milder-mannered individual, she could run out for sundries every now and again; but for anxious hot-tempered Madison, it was a no go. Her anxiety seemed to trigger her new feline form and she didn't exactly need people turning their heads and staring because she was hacking up a hairball every fifteen minutes. She got enough rude stares for her love handles and milkshake thighs and was already self-conscious before the whole "big cat" debacle. Her new ability pretty much guaranteed full shut-in status.

Perhaps she could just pack things up and go to Vegas in search of Siegfried and Roy. They could probably put a fat tiger to work. Or maybe she could meet up with a down-on-his-luck street magician and they could start their climb to the top. He wouldn't even need to learn any magic for the trick to be a success. Vegas sounded too hot and dry for her, but it might be a viable option. She thought the sweating might even help her shed a few pounds.

After dismissing her dreams of a Vegas residency, Madison shook her head and fought for a moment of sanity. Her tiger form had an affinity for ruining her belongings. She was now the proud owner of some newly shredded curtains and an empty fish tank. Despite brushing her teeth several times, she was still suffering from neon tetra fish burps which made her feel guilty about eating Huey, Dewie, and Louie. She assumed her colorful fish hadn't appreciated being a late-night snack.

Nothing about a blind date had seemed interesting and she wished, more than anything, that she'd trusted her gut instincts and stayed home. She looked in the mirror, noting the bags under her eyes, her body reacting from the lack of sleep. She tried convincing herself that turning into a cat was a vivid nightmare. A lucid dream would have been better than being a shape-shifting weirdo. Perhaps her situation was a complete break from reality. It was amazing that the nice men in white coats hadn't hauled her off to the comforts of a round rubber room. Nothing made sense anymore. While she'd never been thrilled with the world, this felt devastatingly wrong.

As she sat, stewing in her misery, someone tentatively knocked on her door. She looked up and yelled, "No one's home. Go away."

But her doorknob jiggled open and Harold stepped through.

"I need to start locking my damn door. Leave. Now. I don't want to see you."

He ignored her, closed the door behind him, and waddled over to a worn recliner before plopping down.

Madison's stomach growled as she folded herself forward, trying to tamp down the pain. She clutched the arm rest of her worn couch while sweat beaded on her forehead. Her disheveled home, usually littered with doom piles and stacks of unread books, looked as if the police had come in and tossed the place overnight. As the wave of pain subsided, she straightened and looked at the object of her hatred. Her affliction had grown more intense since her estranged one-night stand, Harold, had walked through the door.

She glared at the man sitting in her favorite chair. This was all his fault; she'd suspected as much, but his appearance confirmed it. His dismissive, quizzical expression only made her want to slap him. That was, until she gagged on another hairball. Her old stomach ulcers were much better than hairballs, but she didn't really have a choice in that matter anymore.

He had been a Friday night pity fuck. Whether he was the one who had taken pity on her or she was the one that had taken pity on him was inconsequential. She was lonely and horny and he didn't object to getting naked with her.

She should have listened to her mother. "Don't be ridiculously easy all the time," and "You better be able to deal with the consequences of your actions!"

Not that anyone could have anticipated this particular situation; but those words swirled around in her head in her mother's sing-songy "I told you so" tone. Damn her mother for actually giving her some good advice.

"Madison, are you even listening to me?" He shouldn't even be there. The stout balding man was quite possibly the most annoying person—thing—she had ever met.

She stopped rocking on the couch for a moment and looked his way. Lost in her head and wondering if he had actually said something, she spoke. "You know, I don't feel like seeing you right now. I'm quite busy, so if you could possibly show yourself out and jump off a cliff that would be great." She gestured toward the front door. "See? Door. Over there. One foot in front of the other."

"Madison, I think I need to talk to you about some things," he said, clearly unsure of himself and staring at her with wide puppy-dog eyes. "Do you think you could just listen to me for a couple minutes? I promise I'll leave you alone and never come back as long as you let me explain what's happening to you. It's crucial."

She stifled a cough, hoping the hairball had passed. While she's puzzled out parts of her new affliction, she didn't really understand what happened or how she came into this unfortunate state-of-being. She could endure his presence for a few minutes. Perhaps he had some sort of solution or cure for her current predicament.

•　　•　　•

Her overly plucky neighbor and reluctant friend, Sarah, had set Madison up on a blind date, much to her chagrin. Sarah was always sticking her nose where it didn't belong, poking her head into Madison's chronically unlocked apartment and trying to play matchmaker. She'd declined Sarah's efforts over and over and eventually Sarah had put her foot down. She made it clear that non-cooperation was not an option lest Madison be made to submit to something much more mortifying than a blind date.

Sarah strolled along with Madison to the café where she was to meet up with Harold. She didn't trust Madison to actually go on her own—good instincts on Sarah's part.

Harold. Who was called Harold anymore? Really ... this one was going to be a bigger winner than the last one. *Harold is a stupid name—why do I let her drag me into these stupid situations? Harold. Gross!*

Madison had done her best to feign interest in Harold "The Tax Attorney." It was unlikely that she appeared at all convincing, but who would be when forced into a date with schlubby Harold?

The injustice of it all!

By the time they arrived at the café, she was agitated, jaw clenched, and wanting to run. Sarah shoved Madison inside and pointed to the unattractive bald man sitting in the corner.

Great, just great! He was worse than anticipated. *Way to go Sarah ... Do I seem that desperate?*

"Madison, you go in there right now, or else!" she ordered.

"Dude, isn't it bad enough having to see what type of man you think I should be going on a date with? Do I *have* to eat with him?"

"Yes, you moron! You're going, and there's nothing you can do about it. Don't be so shallow. Harold is nice." Sarah snorted with a sense of finality before shoving Madison further into the café, then barricading the door, her small stature never stopping her from a big dramatic gesture.

Madison's eye twitched while she glared at Sarah through the glass before turning around and heading for Mr. Not-Even-Good-Enough-For-Right-Now.

She knew she wasn't all that great to look at. She'd eaten a few too many cupcakes, and it showed right around her twenty-five year old mid-section, but the fact she was chubby didn't mean she should be set up with people like Harold. Maybe someone in the goofy but charismatic category, like Zach Braff or even Kevin James—that seemed right.

She made her way over to Harold's table and sat herself down with a self-righteous thump. "Hey, Harry. Madison. Nice to meet you. How about heading to the bar for some drinks, my treat?"

Harold, taken aback by her abrupt arrival, nodded and the two made a beeline for the door. He followed in her wake all the way down the street to the nearest bar, an Irish themed dive bar whose walls were decorated with old license plates and neon beer signs. It was dark and quiet, and the alcohol was cheap.

"I do actually prefer Harold," he uttered in a voice barely above a whisper.

Of course he did. He was lacking in the confidence department and seeing him, she understood why. Madison wanted to think she was sophisticated and could love a person for their strengths, but she always fell back on a shallow assessment of looks. It made her feel hypocritical, but she did it every time she met someone new. She thought she'd work on it later when she was older and more mature.

Still, Harold wasn't without his charms. Once he loosened up, he was almost witty and after a few drinks his blurred form was near attractive. They played bar dice and Madison laughed at his lame jokes until she was good and hammered. As the night wound down and the sparse patrons stumbled out of the bar, she decided it would be a fabulous idea for good ole' hazy Harry to come home with her. "So, Harry, how about going back to my place?"

Without waiting for his response, she grabbed him by the hand, paid the tab, then ushered him out the door. They caught a cab to her place, buttons popping and hands wandering across each other's bodies on the ride home. The cab driver probably didn't appreciate their sloppy amorous touching, but he never interjected.

Alcohol was apparently a dangerous thing for Miss Madison Murphy.

2

MADISON AWOKE NAKED, her head throbbing with a steady drum beat. Her movements were sluggish and every joint in her body hurt. She'd have believed someone hit her with a car or a train, but in reality she'd only been hit by Harold, who looked like a larger and less green version of a turtle. Him ... and a heavy dose of alcohol. Two-dollar "Wicked Whiskey" was not her friend.

She looked around the room but found no sign of last night's lover. No naked man. No foreign clothes strewn about her room. No smell of bacon and coffee wafting in from the other room. She was smelly, but alone. It took a while before shame set in, but she was glad Harold wasn't in her bed when she woke up. Thank God for small favors.

He did, however, leave a fair amount of "love marks" all over her torso. It seemed that the turtle was more of a hyena in the sack.

She had fragmented memories of her drunken debauchery, which she was thankful for. Remembering a romp with him wouldn't be pleasant in her current condition. She gathered her blankets and sunk back into her bed, not ready to face sunlight or movement when someone rapped on her door with a hard knock.

"Madison, I know you're in there! I want to hear all about last night. I saw Harold rush out of here this morning. It must have gone better than you thought it would. I just knew you'd hit it off."

Sarah, she thought. *Of course, it's Sarah.*

Madison wanted to ignore the door, down a few painkillers and roll herself up like a burrito, but that wasn't an option because Sarah was not going away. She didn't know how she was going to claw her way to her circulation desk job on Monday. She certainly didn't want to talk to anyone right now.

"Madison, you let me in right now! I saw you stumble up here, getting all handsy with Harold last night. I am definitely not leaving until you tell me what happened. I need details, sister."

With a sigh, Madison relented and let her in.

"You know, I knew you and Harold would be a good match, but I didn't expect you to drag him home with you! Good for you. You needed it. So, what was he like? Did you have a good night? And don't even think about telling me that you did not bring him home with you because I saw you from my living room window. The two of you were going at it before you even got in the building ..."

Blah, Blah, Blah. She is not going to shut up until I tell her all about my night with Romeo.

"Uh, Sarah, I barely even remember. We went to the bar and apparently had too much to drink. I have a horrible headache, and he was gone by morning. If you could leave me alone so I can go die in the bathroom, that would be great, okay?"

"Well, then, you don't have to tell me when I'm not wanted. I'll just come back after you're done being a cranky-pants. Good job, though. I'm proud of you for giving Harold a chance." With that, Sarah bounced out the door, a wide smile on her face.

She didn't notice the "side effects" of her interlude until well after the hangover wore off. She lapsed into a day and a half coma, but that too was shrugged off as a result of hard drinking and a night of debauchery with Harold.

She needed recuperative sleep. That and about eight double cheeseburgers from McDonalds. *No joke.*

By the time her painkiller-induced coma ebbed, most of her "love bites" had healed. Which was a plus. Going out in public looking like a patchwork quilt didn't appeal to her at all. She wasn't a teenager anymore and didn't need passers-by deeming her some kind of Hester Prynne. Spying herself in the mirror the way she usually looked was hard enough.

Standing an unimpressive 5'7" and weighing in at about two hundred pounds, her generous size was enough of an attention grabber. She did, however, have some lumps in the right places. Her boobs were okay. If she wore a lower-cut shirt, she thought they distracted from her rolls and jiggles.

She had all but missed the feline whiskers she had grown while she was busy inspecting her body for leftover evidence of her one-night stand. While desensitized to random hairs sprouting on her face, 25 years of being half-Italian had taken care of her concern for an excess of body hair, the long whiskers were an abnormality.

After splashing water on her face, she felt a weighty prickle above her upper lip. Upon noticing the whiskers, she panicked, squealing and falling backwards into her shower curtain. While she didn't fall into the tub and crack her head open, the shock caused her to cough up her first hairball.

"What the hell!" she sputtered after heaving the gooey mass of knotted hair into the toilet. "That is definitely not okay!"

She trimmed off the whiskers, washed her face, then took down knotted her hair, noticing a stark white streak nestled among her usual chestnut brown. Jaw dropped, she blinked twice trying to clear her eyes, before inspecting the white streak further.

At this point, she was beyond freaked out, a familiar panic attack taking hold. Chest pains, cold sweating, and acute, intense nausea. Suddenly, she was in crippling pain, crumpled into a ball on the floor. In horror, she watched her entire body sprout fur, and not "half-Italian fur." Real fur.

As the pain took over, she must have blacked out. What appeared to have been a vivid hallucination knocked the wind right out of her. At first, she was okay with dismissing her panic attack as just that, but the remarkable changes to her body were hard to ignore. She picked up her head and inspected her arms. While her skin had returned to its olive complexion, there were odd clumps of white and black fur on the bathroom floor. She was certain no one had broken in and tossed fur around her passed out form.

Slowly, she pulled herself into a sitting position before bracing herself on the bathroom counter and dragging her body back up. She stood and looked at herself in the mirror. The white streak was still there. She retched when she saw it, certain she was going to cough bile into the sink, a product of her stress or her raging acid reflux. It had happened before. So, she leaned forward waiting for the disgusting fluid to burn its way up her throat so she could cough it into the sink.

Instead. she felt an odd lump rise through her esophagus as she strained for air. Coughing, she felt the lump rise until she was able to spit it into the sink. There was no bile. Madison was looking at a wet lump of undigested fur. *Did I just cough up a hairball?*

Another knock sounded at the door, probably her nosy neighbor again. Still committed to her solitude and figuring out what the hell was going on, she ignored it. She could almost make out muffled words and a masculine voice, but her head was still spinning.

She stumbled to her room, opened her dresser drawer, and pulled out a set of red plaid sweats and an oversized black t-shirt. She pulled them on, trying to comfort herself in any way possible, before walking to the living room and plopping down on the couch.

The knocking returned, more insistent this time. Still, she ignored it. The knob began to jiggle and turn and she cursed herself for being both too forgetful and too trusting to lock the damn door.

Harold walked in and sat across from her like he lived there, making himself comfortable without even asking. There she sat, across the room from prime suspect and enemy number one.

"So, could you run that by me one more time?" she asked, eying the man suspiciously.

"I ... er, may have gotten a little bit frisky with you the other night."

She wanted to smack him. As if his ferocity hadn't been obvious! It sure as hell didn't do much to explain her current condition.

"Madison, you need to pay extremely close attention to what I have to say." He spoke slowly, as if to a small child who could only understand the simplest of things.

"Okay ..." was what she managed to get out for the moment, all ears.

"I bit you the other night, and I shouldn't have done that."

Yeah, she knew that. She shouldn't have drunk until she blacked out or forced herself on him, either, but there was nothing they could do about that now. She was just hoping this guy wasn't gearing up to tell her about his nasty case of syphilis.

"Do you understand what that means?"

"No, you idiot. If I knew what you were trying to say, I would have already tossed you out of my apartment, but there you sit. Unharmed and on my comfy chair." He was really starting to get on her last nerve, and she could feel a slight tickle building up in her throat.

"Okay, well, when I bite someone they don't just scar. My biting you had different repercussions."

She hesitated before responding. *Yep, here comes the syphilis.* "So, you gave me some sort of disease? Great! Please tell me if there's some way to get rid of it? I don't need your weird freaky STD."

"That's not what I meant, Madison. Were you listening at all to what I was just telling you?"

She had tried to listen but found her mind unable to focus. Nerves and anger severely inhibited her ability. "Yes … no … I was somewhere else. Would you mind explaining again?"

"Okay, it's extra important that you listen this time. I'm not going to be around to explain things again. This is the last time you'll see me." He paused to gather himself, "I'm a shifter—shapeshifter, that is. Rather, I turn into a dog during the full moon or whenever I feel the need to get out and run free in the fields."

Trying hard to focus, she struggled to hang on to his words; the man was jumping from regular to freaky-deaky in three seconds flat. "You *what*?"

"I change into a dog, and now—because of my carelessness the other night—you're probably going to turn into one too."

"Cat," she replied nonchalantly.

"What?"

"*Cat*, Harold. I turn into a big jungle cat. Stupid white fur. Stupid white hairballs. Stupid round green eyes. What the fuck, man? You couldn't keep your animal diseases to yourself?"

A shifter.

Madison Murphy—a shapeshifter.

If I have to change shapes at random, why can't I shapeshift into a supermodel instead of a stupid cat?

3

"**M**ADISON? ARE YOU OKAY?** I just came over to help you understand a little bit about what this all means for you."

Well, that was nice of him ... talking as if he wasn't the culprit in the first place! He'd taken the time out of his busy tax attorney schedule to inform her she'd been turned into some supernatural being. Why couldn't she have been turned into some super sexy vampire with flawless skin and a great bod? No, she had to turn into an oversized fat cat who was apparently prone to anxiety-induced hairballs.

She should have been on the defensive when he had showed up on her doorstep, but she'd let him waltz in and sit down anyway. Despite her more sensible nature, she even believed what the crazy little man told her. Though, the physical proof had given her a push in the right direction.

"So, you got any pointers for a young feline on the go?"

"Aside from keeping your temper under control, I can't help you out. Getting too worked up can trigger your change. Try yoga. You'll get used to it after a while. We all do. If it makes you feel any better, I'm being punished for my lack of discretion. We're not exactly allowed to create new shifters without proper consent. This is not a normal situation and I'm sorry. I shouldn't have gotten carried away with you."

"Gross!" She replied, not caring if she hurt his feelings. Their drunken romp left her with enough shame and regret to last her an eternity.

"They're sending me away for punishment, but I can leave you with a friend's number. Maybe he can help you adjust to your new lifestyle. His name is Maxwell, and he works over at Caldwin Brothers Law Firm."

Great ... another attorney.

"Thanks for manning up. I don't have much else say to you, and I don't really want to see you ever again, but it's nice to know I'm not crazy. Or at least I'm not the only crazy person in Wisconsin. I'll make sure to give your attorney friend a jingle if I feel the need to start spraying things. Or wait, is that only male cats? Either way, you'd best be on your way to the punishment chamber. Try not to turn anyone else into a fantasy creature or whatever."

With that, she stood, wobbly on her feet, and shooed him out the door.

Shapeshifter. So, I'm a literal real-life shapeshifter. Lame.

Madison desperately tried to cling to normality, because she wasn't much of a fan of reality at the moment. Reality, as it turned out, was pretty flipping ridiculous. She wanted nothing to do with it. That happy little rubber room sounded pretty relaxing right about now. She flopped back down on her couch after watching Harold walk down the hall and get into the elevator.

"So ... some random man comes into my living room and tells me I'm a shapeshifter. That was it. No take-backs? No do-over? Insane."

She looked at the card Harold gave her and tossed it on her side table. It wasn't as if she was ever going to call this mysterious Max character. Still, she was quite curious as to how many freaks lived in southeastern Wisconsin or the whole of the USA. It daunted her.

"What else did that insufferable man say about my condition? I can't get angry unless I turn into the white furry cat-beast and … something about the full-moon fever. Great, this is just what I need. I couldn't have won some sort of game show or lottery prize instead. Ugh."

It was just Madison's luck that some unwanted and unattractive blind date turned her into a big ol' white Siberian tiger and, to top it all off, her awful white streaky hair aged her in a way she didn't appreciate and wasn't at all ready for. She hadn't expected to need to deal with white hair for at least another decade. White hair in her mid-twenties felt especially cruel.

Feeling a little unprepared for her new situation, she regretted not listening to Harold a little better, but her patience for that man was virtually non-existent. So, now she was stuck.

"What the hell do people … err … shifters, do in this situation? Shouldn't this new lifestyle come with a handbook?" Madison sat, lost in her thoughts for minutes or hours, staring into space and letting time pass her by. She was jarred back to reality by the high-pitched voice of her neighbor.

"Madison, are you in there?" Sarah called from behind the door.

Madison shook her head, letting reality filter back into view. "Yeah, Sarah, hang on a minute." She stood and stretched, her shoulders cracking in the process, before walking towards the door and letting Sarah inside.

Despite her pushy demeanor, she was a "normie," and Madison could use a dose of normalcy. Sarah's extra bouncy golden curls, thin frame, and big doe eyes were usually annoying, but right now Madison craved anything that didn't sound like it had come from a Dungeons and Dragons nerd-fest.

"So … before you say anything about Harold. I want to let you know that we talked it over and decided we're not right for one another. It was a one-night fling, and we're over. Though, he did suggest a friend I may be more compatible with. Max something-or-another. He even gave me a business card." She gestured to the discarded contact information on her side table, certain it would keep Sarah's matchmaking attempts at bay.

Sarah perked up, immediately excited after learning about Madison's new prospect. "So, are you going to call this mystery guy? What's his name? What's he like? Do tell."

"Harold didn't give me many details, just a phone number. He also mentioned something about the Max dude being a lawyer."

"Oooh, another lawyer! Aren't you the lucky girl?" Sarah laughed and elbowed her friend. "Let's sit down and come up with a plan of attack."

"Yeah, lucky, that's it. Unbelievably lucky." Madison said before moving to the couch and sitting with Sarah.

"Well, you should call him, and when you do, you need to tell me all about him. Sneak some pictures if you can or maybe conveniently invite me over when you know he's on his way just so I can scope him out for you." Sarah beamed at her, eyes filled with fiery excitement.

"Sure, Sarah. We can even purchase a spy outfit for the occasion." Madison said, her voice flat.

"Très chic. Can we really go shopping for some spy clothes?"

"Why not, but not today. I'm sort of tired right now. So, if you don't mind, I think I'm going to take a nap." Madison wasn't a fan of conflict. So, she hoped her subtle nudge would register with Sarah.

"Sure, Madison, I'll leave you to it. I'm excited about the new guy, though; make sure not to shut me out of the loop."

"I won't. I promise."

Sarah hopped up and popped out the front door as quickly as she'd arrived. Madison was a little suspicious when Sarah readily agreed to leave. It wasn't like her to miss out on all the juicy details. She should have worried a little more, but her mind was loaded to overflowing as it was. She felt too frazzled to function. So, she went back to bed and slept until morning.

The buzz of her cell phone vibrating against the glass on her bedside table jerked her from her peaceful slumber. Opening one eye, she sighed, realizing she'd slept straight through the night and noticing that blinding sunlight filtering into the room.

Her arm was half asleep and sluggish as she reached out towards the phone and dragged it back towards her head. She answered the call and laid the phone next to her head in the bed, "Yeah?"

"Is this Madison?"

"Uh ... you called me. Shouldn't you know that already?" she asked, half awake, her voice cracking and one eye still crusted shut.

"Madison Murphy?"

"Last time I checked. Who is this, and why are you calling me at such an ungodly hour? I don't enjoy being woken up before ten."

"Sorry about that. Someone by the name of Sarah phoned me and said Harold left you my number."

Sarah's willingness to leave now dawned on Madison—she'd nicked his flipping phone number. "Goddamn it all, that woman cannot keep her nose out of anyone's business. Your name doesn't happen to be Max, does it?"

"Well, it's Maxwell, but Max is also acceptable. So, Harold left you my number, eh? That strikes me as a bit strange as Harold and I aren't the best of ... friends. Inquiring minds and all that."

"Uh, well, this may seem like a strange question. I'm not crazy, at least I don't think I am, but you're not a big cat or something are you?"

"Well, no, most of the time I'm just a regular person. Unless we've been communicating in meows unbeknownst to me."

"Wow, funny guy. Have you ever been a cat? Or maybe ... do you sometimes change shapes?"

"Oh." Madison could tell by his tone of voice that he was frowning. "What sort of trouble has Harold fallen into this time? That man is such a nuisance."

They spent another fifteen minutes on the phone, most of which consisted of Madison explaining her current situation. Turned out, Max moonlighted as a lion—king of the jungle style. He also agreed to show Madison the ropes, figuratively speaking. All in all, he seemed like a decent guy, witty but maybe a little stuffy.

4

“S O, YOU’RE BASICALLY TELLING ME that humans have evolved from many different animals up to and including, but not limited to, wolves, lions, tigers, bears, gorillas, monkeys, large birds, and in some rare cases, rodents?” Madison mused.

“Yes, but mostly we come from some type of monkey. Contrary to popular belief, shifting has nothing to do with ethnicity and everything to do with which animal spirit our ancestors worshipped. Those early tribes were gifted animal senses and qualities many years ago.” Max seemed to be trying to explain as simply as possible, but it was a complicated and unbelievable explanation.

“For example, have you ever seen someone who looked like a rodent? It’s not just the misfortune of the wrong two people mating, but more a dominant trait imbued upon them by an animal spirit, one that never quite disappeared over time. Of course, we’re not all purebred these days, so some shifters wind up as strange hybrid creatures ... a griffin, for example.”

"I see ... Am I supposed to believe all of this supernatural mumbo jumbo?"

"I know this is probably a lot to digest, but since Harold didn't bother to fill you in on several important facts, you're going to have to listen to me a little longer." Max gasped, seeming exasperated.

Harold basically slapped her on the ass and told her good luck, but she was much happier gazing longingly at Max instead of Harold and his sniveling self. In some ways, he did her a favor by rushing off with his sub-par explanation and Sarah's meddling sealed the deal.

Max seemed too broody for her tastes, but his broad shoulders filled out his suit jacket in a way that made her insides tingle. She liked men who were built like refrigerators and Max cut a fantastic figure. However, it wasn't the fact he was 6' 3" or the fact he seemed like he'd be perfectly comfortable sitting at a table full of delicious Vikings that had Madison's head spinning.

Madison had read too many books about roguish types saving damsels-in-distress to not be enchanted by Max's dominant presence and mischievous smile, a half curve, that showed his deep dimples and glittering blue eyes. She had trouble believing he was even real. He could have walked right out of one of Michelangelo's paintings and she'd have thought, *yeah, that's about right.* If he wasn't standing right before her, she'd have expected him to be carved from marble and roped off somewhere like the Metropolitan Museum of Art.

Madison took a moment to ensure her jaw was shut and made her best attempt to not leer at the man. Once or twice she was afraid she'd actually been drooling as she daydreamed about him riding around on a white horse. If he noticed, he kept it to himself. Try as she might, she struggled to pay attention to what seemed like vital information because her brain only cared about what was under the expensive-looking suit.

"... and so, you see, when a human is bitten or scratched by someone infected with the shifter disease, their latent tendencies aren't so latent anymore."

"Wait, can you run that one by me one more time? Is it like catching malaria from a mosquito?"

"That's almost exactly what it is, except instead of malaria, you get shapeshifting abilities. But it doesn't make you a freak, just ... more in touch with your roots. We all have a beast inside, but so few unlock the abilities."

"I guess I'm stuck this way forever then, huh?"

"Maybe reframe that thinking. You've always been a feline on the inside. Now your outsides match."

A week ago, Madison would have peered deep into his sexy blue eyes that crinkled in the corners ever so slightly and thought, *Gee ... it's a shame he's such a loony, because, man, is he a hunk.*

But today ... today she believed every word out of the man's pillowy lips. *Oh, happy day!*

"I'm sorry if I seem distracted, but this is farfetched. I mean, I believe you because I have no other choice, but it's still unsettling. Last week, I was more than content to plop down on my couch, drink a sixer of Miller Light and watch the Packer's game ... but today I'm a page in a fantasy novel. It's too much."

"I understand, and I'm sorry you've found yourself in this situation." He looked at Madison, raising an eyebrow. "I guess when you engaged in sexual relations with Harold, he was a bit surprised and had some trouble controlling himself. I don't think the man has been with a woman in the last eighty years. You've done him quite a courtesy." Maxwell chuckled.

Madison was mortified. Not only was this man unbelievably good-looking, but he knew all about her little tryst with Harold. "Wait. Eighty years? You don't mean that literally, do you?"

"Erm ... yeah, guess I forgot to mention that detail. You must forgive me. The whole, as you say, 'shifter thing' slows down the aging process. How old do you think *I* am?" He grinned.

"Now I'm not so sure; I'd have put you at about thirty-four, but this seems like a trick." The slight wrinkling about his eyes and the pronounced laugh lines in his face coupled with her deductive reasoning had led her to this conclusion. He was youthful and strong but did have signs of aging that Madison's face didn't quite show yet. She knew fine lines and wrinkles were around the corner, but she wasn't there just yet.

"Now, that's a compliment." He chuckled. "I think I'll be 120 or so this year. I've lost track over time, but that's a pretty good ballpark figure."

"Well, hell! I guess I could get into this being a shifter thing. Though the hairballs have got to go. Any other perks come along with this whole weird situation?" This was the first good news Madison had heard. Being twenty-five was great, but being able to stave off the signs of aging was even greater.

"Aside from the odd senses you'll start developing and the stunted aging process, not really. However, since you're a pretty kitty like me, you'll start developing cat-like abilities even while you're in human form … better eyesight, agility. It's really not such a bad deal … and lucky for you, you're not a wolf. They can only shift during the full moon. You have the ability to shift whenever you want, though you *must* shift during the full moon."

Madison scoffed, "Okay, then."

"It just sort of happens, and there's no fighting it. You may, however, notice some unsavory side effects of the shifting process. You're sprouting and shedding fur in a matter of mere minutes, and that can muck up the works, so to speak. You will grow used to it in time."

The hairballs, okay. "Good to know. Thank you so much for taking time out of your day to explain all of this to me, Max. I truly appreciate it; we'll have to do coffee again sometime soon."

Madison tipped her paper cup into her mouth, savoring the last ashy drops of coffee. Caffeine tended to calm her and she needed that relaxation to cope with the extremely odd conversation she'd just had.

She reached out to move in for a handshake, the prospect of touching Max sending giddy waves of nervous energy down her spine.

"I'd prefer a steak dinner, and you're welcome." He winked at her, taking her hand and squeezing it gently.

Did he just wink at me? There was no way that man just winked at me.

"I was quite serious about that dinner. Would you like to dine with me tomorrow evening? I think I can help you with this transition and I would love the company of a beautiful woman."

Of course, Madison was free tomorrow night. She hadn't gone into the library on Monday or Tuesday and was probably fired, and she had no social plans. Harold was the first action she'd had in forever. Her social calendar was dusty and mummified most days. She thought the man was a bit delusional, but she was in no way prepared to turn down his offer. She'd left the house and had coffee with him without any unsavory side effects. She hadn't gotten too agitated. She hadn't spit up hair. She wasn't on the floor in pain while her bones rearranged themselves. So, she thought dinner would be safe too.

"I'm not sure. I'll have to check my calendar, but I'll give you a call later?" She was sure he could tell she was lying, but she didn't want to sound overeager about the encounter.

"I'll be in a meeting this afternoon but leave a message. If I don't hear from you, I'll assume we're meeting at Anthony's Steak House at seven tomorrow night."

"Sounds great."

With that, they parted ways. Madison was both excited and better informed than she had been before meeting the delectable Max. The encounter was a win. She even left their meeting with enough daydreams to rev her engine for days to come. It was a distraction from the troubles of her new affliction and her general state of being. She exited the coffee shop, almost skipping down the road, while wondering what to wear to her fancy dinner with Max. She didn't think she had anything suitable or flattering enough at home and resolved to stop at Torrid for a little black dress.

5

M ADISON RETURNED HOME with two dresses. She wasn't in love with either, but she thought they hid her most unsightly bulges. Black was flattering on everyone and she hoped Max would agree. As she was clumsily digging for her keys, she heard a familiar voice behind her.

"I hear you went on a date with the mysterious Max."

"And, how did you catch wind of that one, Sarah?" She said, feigning curiosity. While Madison was still slightly perturbed with Sarah and her meddling, the prospect of her dinner date with Max dulled the annoyance to a low hum. She finally got her keys in the front door and Sarah strolled in alongside her.

"You know, a little birdie told me ..." Sarah replied, batting her eyes innocently at Madison.

"A birdie, and it had nothing to do with you taking it upon yourself to call Max and make him call me?" Madison scoffed, dripping with as much dramatic flair as she could muster, but a smile still slipped on her lips.

"Oh yeah. That. You don't mind, do you?" Sarah twirled a golden lock in her finger, playing innocent.

"Of course I mind, Sarah. You're just lucky the man was gorgeous and not another toad like Harold." *Well, actually, Harold was a dog.* "You may as well sit down, Sarah. I know you're not going to leave until we talk about this."

The two wandered to the living room and flopped down on the couch, side-by-side.

Madison wondered what kind of animal Sarah would be if she was turned. She was betting on Chihuahua but wasn't willing to sink her teeth into her to find out. "We're going to dinner tomorrow night, if you must know."

"That's so wonderful. It's about time you found someone to appreciate you."

Whether or not that was a backhanded compliment, she couldn't tell. Sarah seemed genuinely happy that Madison was interested in someone of the male persuasion, not that Sarah would have minded if men weren't Madison's thing. She just wanted Madison to get laid and maybe live happily ever after.

For all her poking around, Sarah had a good heart and was truly her most steadfast and tenacious friend, even if Madison didn't appreciate it all the time.

She insisted on having Madison model her new dresses so they could choose one for the outing. Madison begrudgingly agreed and went to her room to slip on the first of the two dresses, a sleeveless black dress with a peplum to hide her belly. She hated parading herself around in front of anyone. Though she had to hand it to Sarah, the woman knew what she was doing when it came to wardrobes, hair, and makeup.

"That's cute," Sarah mused, "but I don't know if it's the one. Go put the other one on and come back."

Madison huffed and went back to her room to squeeze herself into the lower-cut sequined tea dress she had almost left at the store.

Sarah whistled when Madison came back into the room, "That is the one. Look at your breasts. I'm jealous."

The sequined dress did a wonderful job of hiding Madison's unsightly bulges while also highlighting her ample bosom. She expected to look like a sausage about to bust free from its casing, but was pleasantly surprised with how attractive the dress made her appear. She looked good in the store's mirrors, but those were always tricky. Things didn't always look the same when she got them home. This, however, did her body justice.

The outfit was sure to "wow" Max, or at least make him not want to throw up in his mouth when she walked in the room. Having the girls front and center may help distract him from some of her less attractive features, but she worried he'd think she was a tart. Though he *had* distinctly winked at her right before they had parted, and he *had* invited her to dinner. Not that it meant he was interested in her; he could just be taking pity on a pathetic girl in an unfortunate situation. Or maybe he just had an eye tic.

She thanked Sarah for her input and shooed her out the door so she could do her makeup and curl her hair. Once she was satisfied that she looked as good as she possibly could, she gave herself a final glance in the hallway mirror and walked out the door. She caught a cab to the restaurant and stood awaiting her date.

Once Max arrived, the two walked to a small table in the corner of their restaurant, ordered their food, and drank plenty of red wine. Giddy from the interaction, Madison let her self-restraint falter. She laughed as her vision blurred. She felt more out of control than she should have after just a few drinks, but she tried to maintain her composure. She didn't want Max to think she was a sloppy drunk.

.   .   .

Grabbing at her head, Madison felt confused by her surroundings. *Did I overdo it again?* She remembered her date with Max had been going well enough, but there were some blank spots in her memory. Waking up on a cold, hard concrete floor, her dress slightly shredded was a shock. While she'd had a few of these events in the last few days, they weren't normal or welcome. At least before, she'd woken up in familiar surroundings. This was next level.

The large bump on her head suggested that she didn't just black out this time. Rather, something or someone else, had caused her to black out. "Ouch." Her words were sluggish and her tongue felt foreign in her mouth.

When her head fog cleared some, she could make out grimy silver bars in the near distance. She was in a cage or maybe a jail cell; it was tough to tell with blurred vision and a jarring headache. The little floaty spots in her vision didn't help either.

There was, without a doubt, a huge golden lion staring at her from beyond the bars. Max … it must be Max. "Um, Max? Is that you? Good kitty! Did you come here to help me? Where is 'here' kitty? How the fuck do I get out?"

The large cat turned its head sideways to quizzically glance her way before romping away. Either it wasn't Max or much more devious forces were at work.

Is he a serial killer? Of course, he's a serial killer! The wink was just a ruse. *Ugh.* She didn't know who else would know her whereabouts. The lion had to be Max. Sarah knew she'd gone on a date, but she probably didn't whomp her on the head with a bottle and drag her into a dingy jail cell. Plus, the probability of Sarah turning into a beautiful golden lion was slim. She had no feline qualities about her. At all.

That left Max. He'd been cute and charming and maybe that had blinded Madison to his more sinister qualities. She didn't understand why he'd want to hurt her. She hadn't done anything wrong. The date had gone so well. They didn't really even know one another. He seemed so helpful at coffee and was so friendly during dinner, as far as she could recall. She realized they didn't know one another and that he could certainly be a psycho.

She struggled to puzzle things out, but the throbbing pain in her head wasn't helping her sleuthing abilities. She spent some time inspecting her cell. There was no way she could escape. She was much too wide to fit through the bars, even in her cat form, and she wasn't strong enough to bend or break them. She could reasonably squeeze through the window without the bars, but she lacked the reach and strength to do anything about that. She could touch them, but that did her no good. The cinder blook wall at the back of the cell seemed a bit too sturdy for Madison to break through or tunnel under. Something big enough and heavy enough could damage the wall, but in this case Madison didn't qualify.

So, the only choice she had was to sit and wait for someone to let her know what the hell was going on.

She must have stopped paying attention to her surroundings because she snapped back to reality when she heard the jingling of keys from down the hall.

When the perpetrator of the noise got closer, Madison was instantly relieved. It was Max, eyes sparkling and a slight smirk on his face, keys in hand. *Here we go.*

6

"EXCUSE ME, BUT WHAT THE HELL am I doing locked up in a jail cell, and why aren't you helping me?" Some dinner companion he turned out to be.

She should've been suspicious at his cavalier behavior and eager dinner invitation, but she wanted so desperately to believe that someone as gorgeous as Max could be interested in her. She knew they'd gone through a couple of bottles of wine, but the conversation was flowing and she wasn't sure how much she'd actually had to drink. It all seemed so perfect, too perfect maybe. He smiled. He laughed. He joked. He complimented her. She was wrapped up in the fairy tale quality of their night out and never guessed he'd had any kind of ulterior motives.

"Yes, well, sorry about the bump on the noggin and the whole locked up thing, but it's for the best," he responded, amazingly put-together for a man who had just trotted around in lion form looking at her like she was an animal in a zoo. This must have been what her childhood hampster had felt like.

"What the hell are you talking about, tough guy? Since when do fancy attorneys set up innocent women, knock them out, and lock them in cold dark dungeons? Don't you just practice tax law like Harold?"

"I guess since about the beginning of time. Didn't you ever study European history? I never said I was a tax attorney. That's an assumption you made."

"I ... well, okay. Maybe I jumped to that conclusion, but maybe you could have been up front with me about your real motives. I never should have fallen for your silver-tongued act. Why would you want to go out with me anyway? The next time you ask someone on a date, maybe lead with the kinky lock you up in a cage bit. Something like, 'Hey! I'm a psycho killer who plans on making you a prisoner before I cut your fingers off and eat them or whatever.' That would have at least been common courtesy."

"Hey there, missy, I didn't say anything about a date. Though, you do look tasty in your little torn frock. Showing a bit more skin than I find appropriate for a first date, but hey, who am I to complain?" He grinned at her.

Stupid king of the jungle with his arrogant attitude. Madison looked at him, her incredulous expression splattered across her round face. "Well, it would have covered a sufficient amount of skin if someone hadn't gotten me drunk, manhandled me, and tossed me in a cell."

"Who says you were manhandled? It's not my fault you are a lush. Besides, Rocco tells me he treated you with the utmost respect."

"Yeah, sure, whatever, Max. I should've known better than to take a phone number from Harold. He got me into this situation in the first place. Meeting with another someone I didn't know wasn't my smartest decision. Stranger danger and all that jazz."

"I assure you, Madison, that you are in much less danger here than you would be out there."

Madison was confused by his vague proclamations. She didn't know what "out there" meant or why she was in any kind of danger, other than the immediate danger she found herself in. "What are you talking about, you dick? No one out there would lock me up like a criminal!" She rushed towards the bars and reached a hand out, trying to grab Max by the collar and drag him towards the cage. But he stepped backwards and laughed upon her approach.

"No, but they would've killed you. That's for certain, and they sure wouldn't have treated you with the courtesy I'm showing you right now."

"You call this courtesy? I'm dirty, in rags, and locked in a cage, you idiot! What kind of courtesy is this?"

"The kind that keeps you alive." Max shook his head, seeming annoyed.

Madison didn't even bother trying to make sense out of Max's ramblings. He was obviously a loon. Granted, he was an attractive loon with wonderfully wild hair, all tousled and sexy. *Yeech, Madison, the man is keeping you in a cage. Get a hold of your hormones, you dummy!*

"Keeping me in a cage is necessary ... why?"

"It's for your own protection, and if you promise not to run away, I may be persuaded to let you go. You seem like you've sobered up. Show me I can trust you and I'll give you a longer leash."

She felt that familiar itch in her throat and swallowed hard, trying not to wretch up something disgusting in front of him. "Fine, let me out. Now. I'll behave. I promise." Her words dripped with disdain.

"With that attitude, I don't think so. I'll come back and check on you when you've calmed down, then maybe we can calmly discuss setting you free. You'll find a bottle of water in the corner with that crumpled up blanket. Maybe drink it. You're probably dehydrated."

With that, he turned and walked away, keys jingling as his hips swayed down the hallway.

"Asshole," Madison muttered, far from under her breath, but Max didn't bother to pay her any mind. "I'll show him calm.

Locks me up and thinks I'm just going to sit here like a good girl just because he's pretty. Ugh!"

She relented; at least she managed to keep herself under control. She wasn't in pain and turning into a tiger on the floor. As long as she could keep her emotions in check, things would be fine. Madison didn't think her tiger-self would appreciate being caged any more than her human-self did. She didn't want to be trapped like one of those poor zoo animals, serving at the whim of the sloppy general public.

From what she could tell by peering through the small, barred window, the moon wouldn't be full for another three or four days. Spending that long in Max's "five-star suite" wasn't her idea of a great time. His bed, maybe, but that was just the hormones talking.

Madison heard a sound from behind her, something tapping against the window above her.

Tink.

Tink … Tink …

TINK … TINK … TINK … TINK

"What the fuck is with all the clinking, already? Can't a girl get a moment's rest?" Madison screeched at no one, or at least she didn't think anyone was there, until one of those *tinking* pebbles caused the window to splinter slightly. "Ouch! Does the torture never end? Isn't it bad enough I'm locked in a cell, but you have to throw rocks too? Who the hell is out there?"

"Madison?" a timid voice uttered, clearly from outside the building.

Sarah … "Sarah! Sarah, is that you? What the hell are you doing here?" God bless the damn nosy neighbor.

"Madison, what's going on?" Sarah sounded determined but afraid.

"Honey, if I knew that, I'm pretty sure I wouldn't be sitting here on my fanny taking in the beautiful sights of cell block A. Wait. What are you doing here? How did you find me? Are you a part of this mess?"

There was a short pause before Sarah spoke again. "Well, I was sort of following you to your date because I wanted to catch a glimpse of Mr. Wonderful, and when I saw you passed out in some big guy's arms and being tossed into a car, I thought I should maybe call the police or follow you," Sarah explained. She was nosy as all hell, but also quite the clever minx.

"Did you bring the cavalry? Are the police on their way?"

"No ..."

"The Incredible Hulk?"

"Madison, that's ridiculous."

"Keys? Dynamite? Did you bring anything that might be helpful?"

"Well, no ... I didn't exactly stop to pack supplies. I just wanted to find out where they were taking you and to make sure you were okay. I was so worried and didn't think this through."

Sarah's voice filtered through the window and Madison worried someone else would hear but she was also annoyed that Sarah had showed up on her own.

"Locked in a cell here, Sarah ... not okay! Not okay! Someone carried my unconscious body to a random car and you thought there was a chance I'd be okay?" While yelling at Sarah, Madison had to be mindful of her emotions. Pausing to take a few deep breaths, she settled down before something less than savory happened to her body.

"What was that? Are you okay?"

"Yes, I'm fine. Trying not to shift."

"Shift? What are you talking about?" Sarah asked, obviously confused.

"Yeah, long story. So, how do you plan on getting me out of here?"

"Well, I could go around the house and ask that Max guy to let you out."

"Sarah, that's the worst idea I've ever heard." Madison rolled her eyes. "Seriously, he locked me up; he isn't just going to let me waltz out of here. What else ya got?"

"Well, I could just take my car back into town to get the police—"

"*Car*? You brought your *car*? Drive the flippin' thing into the side of the building and get me the hell out of here before they try some weird freaky experiments on me."

"Oh, but Madison, I don't want to chip the paint. It's an almost new car," she whined.

"Sarah, my life is at stake here. Some weirdo locked me in a dungeon conveniently located somewhere in his house. Or–Is this a house? I don't even know. But, I think a chip in your car is the least of our worries. Just smash into the building and get me the hell out of here. If the insurance won't cover damages, I will."

Madison moved as far from the window area as possible, grabbing the blanket on her way. She held the blanket up as a sort of shield, closed her eyes, and prayed to the goddess that she'd be free soon.

Luckily for Madison, Sarah was a bit of a "proactive" driver and it only took her one nice, good smash to break away enough of the window and part of the wall, creating a big enough space for Madison to hoist herself up and skitter through. The car was even still running.

"Hurry, get in before someone notices," Sarah said while glancing around to see if anyone had witnessed the accident.

"Sarah, you just drove a car through the side of someone's house. I'm pretty sure they noticed. Let's get out of here." Madison said, her tone still clipped, "— and thank you."

"Fine, but you have some explaining to do. This stuff doesn't happen to normal people. I have so many questions."

"Deal." Madison replied, opening the passenger door, and jumping into Sarah's car. Sarah threw the somewhat damaged vehicle into reverse before speeding away.

7

S ARAH, MADISON'S PARTNER IN CRIME, was driving merrily down the road and away from the makeshift prison.

"Was there, like, a jail cell in that basement or something?" Sarah asked, her tone far more chipper than seemed appropriate. Her sunny disposition outshone Madison's shitty mood, but she was grateful her annoyingly positive friend had just driven her almost-new car through the wall of a house just to set her free.

"Yeah, that's exactly what was happening down there."

"But, why did that guy wine and dine you just to kidnap you and lock you away like a princess in a fairy story?"

Madison sighed, hoping her friend wouldn't think she was insane, before launching into the whole ordeal. As they drove back towards their homes, Madison regaled her with the story of her unfortunate night out with Harold, her new feline form, and her time with Max.

"Okay, wait. You're telling me Harold was a masterful lover?" She was beyond astonished by that little tidbit. "Hey, if

I had known, maybe I would have hopped into bed with the guy too! Me-ow!"

"That's not the point. You aren't at all fazed by the whole shape-shifting thing? Nothing ... nada ... not even a moment's hesitation in believing me?" Madison knew her friend was odd, but her lack of a reaction here felt wrong.

"Weird things like that happen all the time. Even I have a cousin who's a vampire, don't you?" Sarah said, nonchalantly. She shrugged and went back to glancing at Madison in hopes of more information about Harold's sexual prowess.

"So, you're telling me you've known about this whole supernatural underground for years?"

"Yeah, seriously, you didn't think Stuart Townsend was actually pretending to be a vampire in *Queen of the Damned*, did you? Or Marilyn Manson ... like he's not a demon?"

"For real? You're not just fucking with me because you think I'm a loon, are you?"

"No, I'm completely serious," she stated matter-of-factly. "The only thing I don't get is why hunky Max went and clobbered you and locked you in his dungeon? Maybe he's into bondage? That could be fun. Do you want me to bring you back?"

"I don't think bondage is the answer. I mean, he may be into bondage, we never got that far in our relationship, not that I would be comfortable with getting shackled for fun. It's just not my cup of tea ... but that's entirely beside the point."

Max was a whacked-out psycho and she figured he wanted to kill her, but he was still a hottie, and she was driven by hormones. She hated herself for still daydreaming about his naked body. *Drat.*

"Anyway, Max said I was in some sort of danger, but he wouldn't explain anything to me because apparently my angry disposition displeased him. As if I'd be happy to wake up all battered and in a cage." *Calm down, Madison, calm down. Deep breaths.*

"I wonder what kind of trouble he thought you were in."

"Sarah, he is crazy, a sexy psycho, a sociopathic killer! I doubt I was in any sort of danger aside from the danger he put me in. I mean, why would I be? Ugh ... life is much too difficult. I just want to drink a case of beer and drown my sorrows in a bowl of cheese soup. Is that too much to ask for, beer and cheese soup?"

"Stop being dramatic. You don't know if he's a nut ball. Maybe you really are in some sort of danger? I don't think we should be at home right now. Maybe we should get out of town, rent a hotel room, lay low for a couple of days? We should have gotten those spy clothes!"

"Who says *we* are doing anything?" Madison asked, hesitant to include her friend in her troubles any further than she already had.

"Yeah, like I'm not coming with you. For one, you're pretty much clueless when it comes to the paranormal and you totally owe it to me. I am not going to sit at home wondering what sort of adventures you're off on." She stamped her left foot with a decisive thump, a gesture of finality.

"Adventures! This is my life, not a fairy story. I don't want to go on adventures. I want to put my sweats on and play Nintendo until I'm calm and sleepy. I want to forget that all of this happened."

"Uh, you're so ridiculous. You don't get to just ignore what's going on with you. We're going incognito. Together. I'm coming with you and if you don't like it then you can go back to Max for help."

Madison rolled her eyes, though she regretted letting her emotion show on her face, "Fine, let's go. Where exactly are we going, again?"

"I think there's a hotel off Highway 14, we'll probably be safe there for a while. Though, I don't think we should take my car ... or yours, for that matter. Too obvious."

"Great, now you're a detective, too. Fine, Sarah, you go get us some clothes and things from the Walgreens and I'll call a cab."

"Oohhh, goodie!" Gleefully, Sarah pulled into the Walgreens parking lot. She parked, hopped out of the car, and skipped away, lost in a fantasy. She thought this was a good ol' fashioned buddy adventure, and not a real-life nightmare.

Madison shook her head and grabbed for Sarah's cell phone. Her own had a splintered screen and a dead battery. She called for a car and sat with her head down, trying to figure out what to do next.

•   •   •

"You all set, Madison?" Sarah said, peering through the cracked car window at her friend expectantly.

"Yeah, yeah, I'm done changing." She sighed as she heaved her new duffle bag over her shoulder and clambered out of Sarah's damaged vehicle. "What's even in this thing?"

"I got some extra t-shirts and sweats, undies, snacks, water, and makeup. The basics."

"Makeup?" Madison asked.

"Well, we don't know where we're going to wind up. Just because we're on the run doesn't mean we need to look haggard."

Madison shook her head and the two wandered towards the waiting cab.

The cab driver was an impatient asshole. Though instead of the skinny on-the-go hustle and bustle New York taxi drivers, he was large and sweaty and he smelled of pepperoni pizza and barbeque sauce.

After grabbing the bags and heaving them into the car, sweat began to bead on the driver's forehead. He sat in the car, his perspiration excelling in the process. With all the windows up, it created a less than pleasant atmosphere … though the stench didn't seem to bother him in the least. "So, where you two lovely ladies headed this evening?"

He waggled his eyebrows at them via his rearview mirror.

"Can you drop us off at the Motel 6 out on Highway 14?" Sarah asked.

"Meeting up with some men folk for a romantic weekend, are we?" the cab driver asked with a certain hint of perverse suggestion behind his hoarse voice.

"No, no men folk. Just us gals," she replied.

"Lesbos, nice."

Resisting the urge to kick the back of the man's seat, Madison chimed in, "No, not 'lesbos' but even if we were, it's inappropriate to comment on it. You don't know us. What we're doing is none of your business. Just take us to the damn hotel, you stupid gorilla."

"Ah, man-hating lesbians, then?"

"Dude. Shut up and drive."

They spent the rest of their short ride in silence, the driver occasionally glancing back at them in the rearview and licking his lips. Madison thanked all that was good that Sarah hadn't set her up on a date with this disgusting, round and greasy cabbie because he was the worst.

"Here we are, ladies. That'll be eight-fifty ... or we could forget about the fare and you could just invite me up to observe the night's festivities?"

"Gross!" Madison handed him a ten and slammed the door in his face before following Sarah into the hotel's lobby.

"I got us a double, and they have a hot tub!" Sarah said, her voice exuberant.

"A hot tub, yeah ... like that's exactly what we should be spending our weekend doing. Sarah, sometimes I don't think your brain actually works."

"Hey, what's wrong with having a little fun, even if we are on the run? I'm footing the bill and I like a little spa time every now and again."

"We are not on the run. I'm on the run; you're just a tagalong."

"Have it your way, party pooper. I'm going to check out the indoor pool, and I'll meet you up in the room, okay?"

"Yeah, sure, see you there."

Madison made her way to the stairwell and headed up to the second floor to find their room. The extra weight made her muscles burn as she lumbered up one flight of stairs. Once she made it to the top, she paused to inspect both sides of the hallway, ensuring her relative safety, before stepping into her temporary abode.

Then, everything went black. Again.

8

THE WHOLE BEING CLOBBERED THING was getting old fast. Madison had been knocked out twice in less than twenty-four hours. Her new life was just not cutting it anymore—not that her old life had been cutting it either.

"Ow ..." she haphazardly mumbled while making her way back to the world of the conscious. It was a journey she was less than pleased to take. "Goddamn! Do they really need to keep conking me over the head?"

She was still groggy while opening her heavy eyelids and attempting to bring the world back into focus again. "Wasn't the first time bad enough, Max? Did you have to clobber me again? My damn brain has been damaged enough today. You could have just held a gun to my head while escorting me to your car, but *nooo* that would have been *way* too much work for you. God, you're an asshole."

"Well, Ms. Murphy, you're quite entertaining. Much more than I anticipated."

She didn't recognize the voice this time, though things

were still cloudy, but even though her vision had not quite returned, she knew without a doubt that the man behind the voice was not Max. This new voice was rougher, coarse, like someone who'd been a heavy smoker his entire life.

"Max, eh? I can smell him on you. How is the old chap? Keeping you on your toes?"

Madison replied, her snark in full force, "More like keeping me in his dungeon? Who are you, what do you want, and why is my arm chained to this bed?"

She hadn't been locked away this time. She looked around the room for something that could be useful in breaking free or defending herself. The only thing she spotted was Sarah, unconscious, bound and gagged on a shabby hotel chair.

"Well, Ms. Murphy, if you must know, I am an entrepreneur here to offer you a new and exciting career."

Her head swam but her vision cleared enough to make out the man across from her. He wasn't unattractive. He looked dangerous, like a fancy old-timey criminal in his brown suit and pork pie hat.

"You had to knock me unconscious and cuff me to my bed because ...?"

"I figured you'd be much more willing to listen to my proposal without the distractions of movement and freedom." He shrugged.

"Well, aren't you a considerate fellow?" Madison glared in his direction, using her free hand to hold the throbbing spot on the back of her head.

"I do try, Ms. Murphy."

Someone cleared their voice from the corner of the room. She had noticed Sarah's passed out form, but failed to see the two large scruffy men standing post at both of the room's exits—hallway and balcony on the opposite side.

Wonderful. Madison had two psychos and hired muscle on her tail. Not to mention the added stress of having to save her nosy neighbor. She did owe Sarah one heroic rescue and it was looking like she'd be getting her chance sooner than later.

This week just kept getting better. "Are Guido and Nunzio over there really necessary … what did you say your name was again?"

"Frank and Bobby, yes, and I didn't happen to mention my name … yet. I do hope you'll find our hospitality comforting, Madison."

The man's cold demeanor set her off. Her rage rose quickly in her throat as she lost control of her emotions and sputtered until a fully formed hairball emerged. It'd been rumbling around inside of her for a while, waiting for an opportunity to burst forth from her mouth with a disgusting wet hack.

She spat it to the floor before responding to the infuriating man in front of her. "Hospitality? You call handcuffing me to the bed of a hotel room that we paid for, hospitable? I'd hate to see what you consider to be rude."

"I'm sure hate would be the least of your worries if you found yourself in a situation that displeased me."

"Get on with it. What the hell do you want, guy?"

"As I said before, I have a unique business opportunity for you."

"Yeah, well, sorry, but I've got a job. Or, I had one until very recently. I've probably been fired by now. The library is pretty forgiving, but I have probably pushed those limits. Still, no thanks and go away."

"Dear Madison, it's not all that easy. You see, you are quite the find, and I am not the only man hunting for you. Much worse creatures will come in time. In fact, my proposition is downright pleasant compared to what my less-than-reputable brethren would do to you." He grinned at her like a man in charge.

She loathed the prospect of more dangerous men, ones less savory than the mystery man who'd trapped her.

"I think I'll take my chances," she replied matter-of-factly.

"That is a mistake I am not willing to let you make. You see tigers, such as yourself, are a rare find. White ones are rarer still. Your parents must have come from a Siberian or Bengal to produce such an anomaly. As most shifters turn out to be of the monkey persuasion, felines are a hot commodity. You're a very threatening prospect to many shifters out there, and lots of people don't want the balance upset by the introduction of a new power player."

"Power player." Madison clenched her jaw before frowning and wondered if all shifter folk were lunatics. Every single one she'd med so far had been dramatic. "Listen, whatever your name is, a few days ago I was just a regular person. A happy Wisconsin girl wanting to head to Milwaukee to take in a ball game on the weekend before heading back to my tedious day job and somewhat drunken nights. I have no idea what you're talking about. I am no 'power player,' and I just want to be left alone."

Sarah grumbled in the corner, apparently fighting her way back to the world of consciousness. The meatheads stood as silent guardians.

Mr. Question Mark sidled a bit closer to Madison. "My dear girl, there is much you do not understand about our ways. Feline shifters not only have the ability to change into their animal, but they take on their strengths while in human form."

"Yes, I've already been informed."

The man's eyebrow perked at her statement, but he said nothing to clue her in as to why he found this information so interesting. "Ms. Murphy, have you also been told that feline shifters are the only ones to inherit this ability? The old feline gods were the strongest. The dogs, monkeys, and rodents of the shifter world have the ability to shift at will, and the wolves only shift during the full moon. There are other less impressive sorts, birds and bats and foxes. No one really cares about them. You, though, are quite special, and your talents are both coveted and feared in the shifter world."

Madison raised her eyebrows, surprised by this revelation. "Well, no, I didn't know that part, but I don't see how that makes me a threat to anyone. I have no idea what I'm doing half of the time, and I didn't know anything about this whole paranormal subculture until you crazies started explaining things to me. I would've been content to remain ignorant to everything and go on my merry way, even if it meant coughing up the occasional hairball." She was at her wits' end with all these crazy shifters.

"Ah, but like I said before, even if you are not interested in us, we have more than a passing interest in you. There are people who would rip you to shreds on sight. Fortunately, I am not one of those people. I would like to handle this situation in a different manner." The man had a sharp look about him, pointy, hardened, and quizzical.

Madison had no choice but to listen to what he had to say. "I would like to ... recruit you. You see, I am a purveyor of fine shifters. My guards, for example, are both cougars. I, myself, am pleased to be a mighty lion. We, my merry little band and I, are all feline shifters, and I would like to invite you to join our crew."

She took this information and chewed on it. It might be handy to have like-minded "professionals" surrounding her, but something in her gut made her dislike the man who had yet to introduce himself. She didn't think throwing her hat in with a group of feline thugs would be in her best interests.

"Arthur Mainfield," he announced, as if reading her mind.

"Well, Mr. Mainfield—"

"Arthur, I insist."

"Well, Arthur, you present a very interesting case. I would be lying if I said this hasn't been an informative little visit, but what exactly is it that you want me to do?"

"It's just a little reconnaissance work and for you to use of some of your unique persuasive skills."

"You want me to be a spy slash enforcer? I don't think that's my cup of tea. I'll pass, and you can take your muscle and get out of my room." Madison was doing her best to keep her anger under control to avoid another ... incident. The stinging pain in her throat served as an excellent reminder to keep her temper subdued.

"Oh, Ms. Murphy, you misunderstand. This really isn't an offer you can refuse. Aside from the fact you're shackled to the bed, we've also taken the liberty of inflicting your little friend with the shifter disease. Unless you want her to have a rude awakening, you best sign on with us."

Madison reacted with false horror. She hadn't anticipated Mr. Mainfield's strategy, but he also did not know Sarah. While she would not be amused with her new affliction, she would be intrigued, morbidly curious, and in the end likely wouldn't mind all that much. She already knew more about the paranormal world that Madison did.

While what these strange men-beasts had done to her friend horrified Madison, she was also excited to see what kind of animal Sarah would turn out to be. Hopefully, it wasn't a Chihuahua as Madison had guessed earlier because a Chihuahua wouldn't be a very helpful player in an escape plan.

"The damage is already done. There's no going back once you've been inflicted. So, what does it matter? I am disinclined to acquiesce to your request." Madison grinned, taking a quote from the *Pirates of the Caribbean*.

"I am sorry to hear that." Mainfield's goons closed in and threw a black bag over her head. She couldn't see what was happening to Sarah, but at least this time she wasn't unconscious.

9

MADISON KICKED ABOUT in the back seat of the vehicle, squirming for freedom, until someone thwapped her on the hip with something cold and hard.

An unfamiliar voice yelled her way, "Stop moving, and keep quiet or I'll hit you harder next time."

She tried to count the seconds, thinking that may be important to calculating a location. She didn't know how to do that, but needed to focus on something. After a while she lost count, eventually drifting off to sleep.

As she fought her way back to consciousness for the third time, groggy from her unintentional nap. Eyes open, she started into darkness. Something was still covering her head. That didn't give her much of a way to gain a handle on where she was or who she was with, though she did notice someone was carrying her, perhaps to another vehicle.

She was thumped down onto a soft seat and heard the distinct sound of a car door closing. She was definitely riding in the backseat of a vehicle. She could hear noises she wasn't accustomed to—trains, planes, honking horns, the hum of neon lighting. She wondered how much she could hear if she really put her mind to it. These feline senses were no joke. The sounds made her think she was somewhere in the middle of a big city ... Milwaukee or Chicago, perhaps? She wasn't sure how much time had passed since her most recent kidnapping. So, she couldn't be sure exactly where she was.

She hoped she hadn't been asleep long enough to get much further than the surrounding cities. Chicago was even a bit of a stretch as it was about two hours by car. If she'd been riding around longer, then she could be anywhere from the Twin Cities to Dubuque or even Indianapolis by now.

She knew the full moon was only two days away, and she couldn't afford to be caught in the middle of a big city when the shift overtook her. She wasn't sure if it would be different than the times she forcibly shifted before. Being in a big city, she felt like she'd be noticed. She didn't want to get poached on her first night out, and she didn't want to accidentally eat someone. *Do shifters eat people?* Madison's head pounded, as was to be expected, what with all the lumps on her head.

"Where are we?" she mumbled.

"Chicago, Western Avenue," she heard a familiar voice utter from the front seat.

It was not the condescending voice of Mr. Mainfield, and she had never heard his lackeys talk, so they were also out. The voice was distinctly male, which ruled out Sarah, as well. Leaving her with the cab driver, Harold, and Max to choose from.

"Max?"

"That's my name."

"Where the hell is Sarah? Where the hell are we ... and where the hell did you come from? Why is my face still covered? What is going on?" She was near-yelling as rage began to fill her body.

"Sarah, your friend who called me the other night? Why would I know where she was? And, we're in Chicago—I already told you that—and I'm pretty sure I came out of my mother's no-no parts." The sly smile was evident in his glib voice. *Douche bag!*

"Yeah, you're a whole lot of help. God, why couldn't you just leave me tied to that bed?"

"I can tie you to another bed if you wish."

Max reached back towards here and pulled the covering off her head. As her eyes adjusted again, she caught another distinct wink from Max through the rear view mirror. The man was vexing.

"Of course, that's exactly what I want you to do. I'm not thinking about anything but you tying me to a bed and having your way with me. Get over yourself."

"My dear Madison, don't kid yourself. I know you hesitated a moment there when I suggested bondage. It's okay, I'm pretty irresistible ... And I never mentioned anything about having my way with you," he paused for dramatic effect.

Despite everything, his less than subtle advances were working, though Madison didn't want to let that show. She made sure there was a grimace on her face.

"God, you're a pig," she replied, indignant despite her arousal.

"No, I'm a lion. I thought we had already established that."

"How did I even wind up with you? I mean ... one moment Mainfield's henchmen were bagging my head and the next moment I wake up in the backseat of your car?" She threw up exasperated, tied-up hands, furious with the situation in which she found herself.

"Would it have made you feel better if you had woken up naked in the backseat of my car? Because I can arrange that if you want."

"Are you ever serious? I want to know what happened to my friend and how I got here," Madison stomped her foot decisively, and wore a frown to show the seriousness of the situation.

"You're hurting my feelings, Madison. I thought I meant more to you than that. You're just using me to get information. I thought you would at least use me for my body," As he finished speaking, he unbuttoned the top few buttons of his shirt.

Is he doing this on purpose?

"Yeah, well, that could have worked out if you hadn't locked me up in a jail cell, you creep."

"As I said before, it was for your own protection, and if you still don't believe me, then maybe all of those knocks about the head have affected your brain capacity." A hint of frustration at last crossed his perfect face.

"I can think just fine, thank you. Can you please tell me what happened back there and why you've taken me to Chicago?"

"Well, there was no other girl when I showed up to save the day. There were a few dumb brutes, and I bested them with my superior strength, sheer masculinity, and handsome face ... that and Rocco's help, but he wasn't fortunate enough to make it out."

"Okay ..." Madison was waiting patiently, but her patience ran thin.

"We're in Chicago because I have a condo here, and we're going to bunk down until I decide what to do with you."

"But you have to get Sarah! We have to save her." Sarah had saved her life; she was a solid friend who needed help and Madison wouldn't let up until she was safe again.

"She didn't happen to drive into my house earlier, did she? Either way, she wasn't there. So, we really don't know where to find her or even if she is worth finding."

Madison fumed at that. She believed all people were worth trying to save. "Of course she's worth finding; she's my stupid nosy best friend who's always trying to fix me up with unsuitable men. She's just been infected with the whole shifter thing. She's probably scared and alone, and we need to go get her."

"While that's interesting, we can't just run out guns blazing. Let's get to my place, cozy up, have a little sex, and decide what to do from there."

"Excuse me, what? In your dreams, pal." Madison's pulse raced at the idea of getting naked with Max, but she was standing her ground.

"It *is* in my dreams, nice of you to pick up on that. How about we turn fiction into fact?" He turned off his headlights as he pulled into the driveway of a ritzy high rise. The building looked daunting. Max reached back and used his hands to break her bindings.

"What? How? How did you do that?"

"I'm strong. What can I say." He flexed his arm for effect.

"Cool story. Ugh." Madison did her best to comb through her hair with her fingers as she stepped out of the car. Max was already outside and waiting for her.

An eager valet walked out of the double-doors at the front of the building, greeted them, and took the car keys. Another enthusiastic employee held the door open and tipped his hat their way as they entered. He scrutinized Madison's disheveled Walgreen's clothes but didn't say a word.

"Well, Mr. Moneybags, nice digs." Madison was a bit astonished by the rich décor. The building lobby featured a humungous ornate chandelier and several statues of women in various states of undress. It would have been pornographic if not for the artistic value of the works. Madison found them fascinating and would have loved to investigate more under normal circumstances. She began to come around to the idea of hanging around with Max a bit longer. At least long enough to shower and change into something less shabby.

"I try." Max replied, watching Madison take in the ornate surroundings. "Should we get naked now, or after we get up to my apartment?" he asked, before giving her a tiny shove into the elevator.

10

M ADISON WAS ANGRY WITH HERSELF for many reasons. She should abhor the man she shared an elevator with, but she was still salivating over him. He had a confidence that wasn't at all arrogant. Sly, but not arrogant.

Not being able to hate the man who had locked her up should infuriate her, but she couldn't muster the rage. His thick, tousled hair formed a magnificent mane to frame his perfect face. His dimpled cheeks, twinkling eyes and full sexy lips would make any woman drool. That he was so immense in size made her weak in the knees. She felt like a stupid love-sick highschooler in his presence.

She tried to make herself feel better by rationalizing her reaction. *Any woman who didn't go weak in the knees while gazing upon Max's sexy visage was blind.* She firmly believed that even if someone preferred a thinner man or no man at all, the guy was something to behold. Most people could appreciate that he was aesthetically pleasing and kind to the eyes.

She didn't want him to turn her on. She didn't want him to rescue her. She didn't want him, period. Well, maybe that last one was a bit of a stretch.

She wanted him far more than she was willing to admit but was trying to hold onto her denial. It wasn't like she was in love with the man, but she did swoon quite frequently over him.

"Um ... Madison, you can get out of the elevator now. I mean, if you want to keep staring at the dark spot in the carpet, that's fine, but I assure you, my house is much more comfortable ... and there's a bed." He winked again. The man must be a compulsive winker.

"Oh, yeah. Sorry about that, I was just thinking about how much I hate you." Her voice betrayed her lie, but she also didn't need to give him any more encouragement.

"Yes. I'm sure." He glanced back at her while finagling the lock to his apartment.

The door opened to reveal the most extravagant room she had ever seen. It was both homey and elegant. The only thing his living room lacked was a bearskin rug, but considering the duality of his nature, she didn't blame him for not wanting to walk all over one of his fallen brethren.

Perhaps the most overwhelming aspect of Max's house was how well it highlighted his sexy, confident personality. Madison would have doubted that he was the type of person to decorate his own house, but upon seeing it, she wasn't so confident about her musings.

"Madison? You can come in, you know. You don't have to stand in the doorway all befuddled and lost." He chuckled, eyes gleaming in amusement. "Maybe I shouldn't have knocked you about earlier; you're more spacey than you were when we met."

She stepped inside, then pulled the door closed behind her. "What do you expect from me, Max? A person can only take so much in a day."

"Technically, it's been a few days, Mad, but who's counting?"

Mad, she thought. It was an interesting nickname. She wasn't sure if she loved or hated it, but it seemed like a term of endearment.

"Besides you, no one. Seriously, I am so stressed out right now. I'm not coughing up hairballs every five minutes, which is great, but I assure you, I'm at my wits' end."

"I didn't know your wits had an end. I'll try to take it easy on you ... unless you ask me to make it hard on you." He snickered again.

The man obviously thought himself hilarious.

Madison knew shouldn't let herself get lost in his beautiful eyes. "I've got no fight in me right now, Max. Can you just explain what the hell is going on? No tricks this time, ok?"

"Yes," he sighed. "This might take a while. Let me go make some coffee and we can have a little chat."

He went about his coffee making, which amused her. She hadn't pegged him for someone who would know his way around a kitchen, but he was, thus far, full of surprises. Some of them weren't so great, but nobody was perfect. He returned with two steaming mugs of cinnamon coffee with just a hint of cream.

Madison had taken a seat on his leather sofa and he joined her upon his return.

"Are you ready?" He asked, seeming sympathetic and genuine instead of his usual cocky self.

"Yes."

"Madison, you were 'born' in a time of territorial power struggles between the shifters. The entire paranormal world is in upheaval. As a whole, shifters aren't an organized or reformed sort, and right now, they're letting their base instincts lead the way."

"You're not?" She asked, thinking he may need to examine some of his own recent actions.

"If I was letting my primal instincts drive, we'd be in bed by now, but we're not, are we?"

Madison scoffed. "Well, I'm glad I have a say in the matter. Anyway, that's not what I meant."

"I know, but I do so love watching you get flustered."

Heat infused her cheeks. "Asshole."

"Sometimes. But to answer your question, I'm sort of like the Robin Hood of the shifter world. I don't exactly rob from the rich and give to the poor, but I have noble intentions and my band of merry men share my sentiments."

"Okay, and what about the other guys?"

"In case you've forgotten, you were in the company of Arthur Mainfield. He is more of an Al Capone. Juice loans, assassins, spies ... all of that jargon, and he certainly wanted to use you in order to make a power play and reign over all of us shifters. There are other dangerous men out there already planning to eliminate you, because, as you've presumably guessed, you're a rare and precious find."

"So, it seems. So, it seems. You really were trying to keep me safe before, weren't you?" Madison wasn't sure if she trusted him. She knew she was blind to some of his actions because he was a total babe. But, this time he seemed honest, sincere even.

"That's what I said, isn't it?"

"And the cage was necessary because ... you thought I could overpower you with my brute strength or maybe because I'm extra sexy you didn't want all of the other kitties catching my scent and coming to take advantage me?" She knew provoking him was a bad idea, but her anger was getting the best of her.

"You were in the cage because I expected you to react with anger, and I didn't want an angry Siberian tiger tearing through my home."

"Oh."

"But you do make a valid point—you are quite a fetching woman. I can't bat all of the suitors away by myself."

"Would you stop complimenting me already? I know I'm not beautiful, I'm not even pretty. I'm lumpy and frumpy, and I don't need you to patronize me. Seriously."

"But I'm not ..." He looked crestfallen, searching her eyes with his own.

Madison cut him off with a wave of her hand before he could finish. She didn't want him to take pity on her as she had on Harold. Never confident in her appearance, compliments made Madison nervous and overwhelmed. She didn't understand why a man like Max would want anything to do with her. She wasn't rich or beautiful or talented.

Max moved in closer. "Madison Murphy, you exceed the standards of today's society, and if you can't see that, you're blind." He took her hand and absentmindedly stroked it. "You have amazing gold-flecked green eyes. In fact, I've never seen eyes quite like yours before. They're wonderful. Your long wavy hair really compliments your round cherubic face, and your other assets are quite admirable too. You're fetching in a way I can't describe. You really don't see that, do you?"

"Yeah, Okay, then. I appreciate your load of crap, but I am none of those things." Madison had no idea how to react to such wonderful compliments, as she had never been complimented like this before. Not ever. As a child, people made fun of her nose. As a young adult, they made comments about her increasing weight, the jiggle of her thighs, her thick arms. Her mother often likened her to a rolly-polly hot dog.

"You're near angelic in appearance, like the soft women of the Middle Ages, round doe eyes and a substantial bosom, everything you see in paintings that hang in today's art museums. You've stepped right out of time." That last part came out in an almost growl. "You don't take compliments well, do you?" He raised his eyebrow at her once more, an inviting gesture.

Madison was amused that he'd likened her to artwork. Her first impression of him was that he'd make a fetching statue and should be displayed in an art museum. It was an entertaining coincidence. Still, she couldn't believe the things coming out of his mouth. She didn't know what to do with his words.

"No, I don't enjoy compliments based on the fact they're not true. So, either save them for someone who deserves them or compliment me on something realistic. Like my winning personality."

"Ha. You're a peculiar woman, you know that right? I can't say your personality is winning, per se. But you do delight me with your quips and blatant sarcasm."

"Thanks."

"I'm not sure that qualifies as a compliment. I just want you to know I mean everything I said to you. I'm not just trying to butter you up so that you'll join my merry little band; I honestly think you're beautiful."

Max didn't give Madison the chance to debate. He rose and grabbed her arm, pulling her up and towards him, capturing her in a tight and surprising embrace. The determination in his face brought a heated, embarrassing fluster of arousal to Madison.

He pressed his palm to the back of her neck, brought her face to his, and kissed her hard on the mouth.

Her arms flailed as she pulled away from his warm embrace. "Stop it!"

"Madison, shut the hell up before you ruin this moment." He grabbed her again, kissing her deeply and well. This time her lips parted under the pressure of his crushing kiss, allowing him entry, and as their tongues entangled, Madison let out a soft, satisfied murmur of pleasure.

The next thing she knew Max was carrying her into the bedroom. "Well, hell Max, one little kiss, and you think I'm going to sleep with you."

"Yes, yes I do." He replied, kicking the door open and walking over to the bed.

"Stop it. You're going to drop me."

"I will not. Quit ruining the moment."

He laid her on the bed and stared at her curvy body, making her feel exposed and uncomfortable. She looked at him, his arousal obvious.

"Madison, if you don't have anything good to say, don't say anything at all."

He held one of her hands and raised it above her head, pinning it to the bed while his other hand went lower to find the exposed flesh of her hips. As he lightly ran his finger in circles around her soft belly, he smirked. That devilish grin giving her a preview of what was to come. He began inching his palm up across her ribcage and toward her breasts. Stopping just short of the peaks on top of her mounds, he paused to touch his lips lightly to her ears.

He whispered gentle kisses on her earlobe before tracing his tongue down the rim of her ear, her neck and down to her sensual collarbone, sucking hard at the skin in the hollow.

His palm snuck up to her breasts and tentatively grazed the flesh he was not shy about wanting to devour. Her nipple responded, hardening from his probing as she let out another wanting sigh. He ripped off her clothing and kneaded her exposed breast. Flesh-to-flesh. She arched her back, bringing her breasts closer to his moist lips. She sensed his deep primal hunger wanting to take over and maul her, but he remained in control and proceeded with his slow assault.

Madison, however, wasn't actually in control of her feline hormones. She rushed her hand to his waist to unfasten his pants, which she shoved down using her feet. The shirt was next, up and over his head, leaving them both naked atop his bed, bodies intimately pressing against one another. She knew she shouldn't be doing this, but it felt too good for her to actually care.

His glazed eyes met hers, and she could swear that the pupils went vertical for a moment. His probing gaze felt like he was just making sure that she was still a willing participant; something in her feral nature told her he was asking for permission.

She didn't want him to stop now. "Finish what you started, or else."

"So delicately put, but you don't have to tell me twice." Any hesitation he had left evaporated, and Madison gave in to the pleasure of the moment.

With renewed confidence, he explored her breast while his hands moved lower to knead the flesh of her soft hips and buttocks. He nipped at her nipple then returned to her mouth while moving his hand toward her awaiting treasure.

His strong fingers teased her delicate folds. Madison let out a feral moan and parted her thighs to allow him better access. His grin made her think he was up to something nefarious.

He feathered his fingers over her so lightly he barely made contact. Still, it set her desire on fire.

She could sense his concentration; he teased her on purpose. "God, you're an asshole, Max."

"I know, but you like it and don't even try to tell me you don't."

Infuriated and seeking release, she growled at him. He pressed his lips to hers while continuing his light assault on her intimate parts. His fingers finally found her clitoris and rubbed vigorously while she bucked at his sudden assault. He brought her within an inch of release then stopped.

Her trembling form, suddenly robbed of delights, she snapped, "What, that's it?"

"I haven't even started," he replied, his deep voice husky with desire.

Madison's lips curved into what she hoped was a mischievous smile. "Neither have I."

11

THIS TIME, HIS TECHNIQUE was different than Harold's. Hands roamed all over her naked form, followed by little kisses in a trail all the way across her flesh.

Madison's fingertips delicately walked across the wide expanse of Max's chest before following his treasure trail all the way down to the prize. His cock was at full mast while she tentatively played with the hair around his groin and gently cupped his full balls. When her hand finally grazed his hard shaft, he let out a long moan and grabbed her to shift positions.

On top of her again, with one hand on the mattress supporting his weight, he bent down to kiss her full on the mouth. His swollen cock teased her entrance, the head brushing her moist clit a few times before entering her with one swift thrust.

Madison raised her hips hard against him, wanting the invasion to proceed. His tongue hungrily thrust inside her mouth as his hips moved in tune to Madison's urgings. He pulled her harder against him with each powerful thrust.

The pleasure slowly built inside Madison and it would only be a short time before she came. He stopped abruptly and smirked at her.

"That best not be it, Max."

"Not even close ... well, maybe close."

"Um ... I'm ... wait—" He thrust hard into her before she could finish her sentence, which drove her crazy.

A loud wanting moan escaped her mouth before she settled back into the rhythm of his strokes. Max smiled down at her and with one final thrust, as she bucked wildly against his hips, throwing her head back in pleasure. She let the fire of her orgasm consume her as she throbbed around Max's full cock.

A moment later, he climaxed, and they collapsed together in a big sweaty pile on the bed. They lazily draped their limbs over one another and drifted into a light doze.

Madison awoke first. She covertly jabbed a finger into Max's ribs before closing her eyes and pretending to sleep.

"What the ...?" he mumbled.

"Huh? I see you're awake."

"Yeah, it seems that way, eh?"

She caught a glimpse of his back. She had left a few scratches while they were in the throes of passionate lovemaking. The wounds had grown into puffy red welts. "Uh, Max ... I think I may have been a little too feisty with you."

"So it seems."

"Since I'm a shifter and I scratched you, does that mean you're going to turn into some sort of liger?"

"What the hell is a liger?"

Madison rolled her eyes, disappointed with his ignorance.

"You know, like Napoleon's favorite animal?" she said matter-of-factly and perhaps with a bit too much of a cocky undertone.

"Bonaparte?"

"No, Dynamite. You've never seen *Napoleon Dynamite*? His favorite animal is a liger ... half lion, half tiger, bred for its skills in magic."

"I see. Well, that's not how it works, anyway. I'm a lion, you're a tiger. Though if we ever had cubs they'd probably be, how you say ... ligers?"

"Cubs?"

"Um ... long story. I'd rather not explain the particulars right now. Can't we just bask in the afterglow a bit longer?"

She smiled and drifted off once more.

12

MADISON SHOT UP IN BED. "I am such an asshole! We've been here having a grand old time and indulging in the pleasures of the flesh and Sarah is still out there by herself. I am incredibly inconsiderate; we have to save her."

"How much do you know about this Sarah, anyway?" Max asked.

"Well, she's been my nosy matchmaking neighbor for about three years now. She's always in my house pestering the shit out of me. I'd say I know her pretty well."

"How do you know she's not working with Mainfield?"

"She came and saved me from your dungeon, for one."

"Which led you to get captured by Mainfield. So, that's not actually a valid point for me. Plus, she drove her car into my house. What kind of person does that?"

"The kind who's willing to save her friend from an egomaniacal lunatic."

"Madison, I thought we were past that point."

She frowned, no longer certain of Max's intentions. *Why would he make Sarah out to be a bad guy?* "Yeah, I guess not."

He looked wounded. Perhaps she had misjudged the situation.

"I'm just trying to make sense of the situation. We don't want to walk right into a trap, do we?" Max asked.

"Um ... no? I don't think so. I'm sor..." She hesitated, not actually wanting to apologize for her distrust.

"What would Mainfield want with Sarah?" Max said while scratching at his chin.

"To hurt her, to hold her hostage ... I don't know. All of this is still new to me, and I'm not sure how to make sense out of anything." Madison broke down into sobs, tears trailing down her face.

"Madison, don't worry. We'll get this situation taken care of, and if saving Sarah means that much to you, then that's what we'll do." He reached over and placed a warm hand on her shoulder, letting it linger for a moment before starting work on his plan.

Max sprang into action and made a few phone calls, presumably to his brothers (or sisters) in arms. "I have a few friends who are going to case Mainfield's haunts to see if we can figure this thing out."

"So, we're just going to sit here and do nothing." Madison wiped a tear from her face.

"No, we're going to act as soon as we know what to do and where to go, but for now we just have to sit tight, okay?"

"Okay." She sniffled, attempting to regain her composure.

"Unless you want to have another go?" He smiled, a devilish expression on his face.

Madison smiled in kind. "In your dreams, big guy."

"Yes, it will be. Every night."

"Ugh ... gross!"

"That's not what you were saying a few hours ago."

Madison felt her face flush. He was right. He knew he was right; she knew he was right. So, she sat, defeated. "Hey Max, can I ask you a question?"

"Sure, as long as it's not too personal."

"What the hell is your last name?" She felt like a tramp. First, she got down and dirty with Harold, the tax attorney, then hopped into the sack with Max, whose last name she didn't even know.

"Ha. I guess our relationship is far enough for me to divulge that intimate detail."

"I think your intimate detail was just inside of me, so could you just answer the question?"

"King. Max King."

She laughed. "Seriously, your name is Max King? Max King the Lion. That's awesome. How come you lions get such cool names? Arthur is a lion too? Yeah? He has to be with a name like Mainfield ... that's just unreal."

Max nodded. "I told you we were fated to be kings. I guess that's just another reason to support my explanation."

"So, how come I don't have a cool tiger name? Madison Murphy, Siberian Tiger, doesn't exactly sound like a proper tiger name." She pouted, one of her automatic responses to situations she found displeasing.

"I'm not sure, perhaps your ancestors changed the name to fit in. I think Madison Murphy is a perfect name for a tiger, though I've never met a tiger before."

Shocked, it took her a moment to reply, "... Wait, what? You've never met another tiger?"

He rattled off a list of creatures, counting them on his fingers as he went, "Lions, bears, monkeys, apes, cougars, wolves, hawks, and the occasional sewer rat, but no tigers. When I told you that you were a find, I really meant it. Tigers are outrageously rare."

"So, folks are gunning for me, because I'm the only tiger around?"

"That's part of the reason. Your feline abilities make you a great asset because you've got better sight than most people. You have the ability to be sneaky, agile even—as you've managed to prove in bed." He winked.

The man was a winking fiend. Madison didn't blush; she'd grown used to the flattery. That or she was at long last cracking up. "So, I'm like, a super shifter? That's pretty cool."

She let it all sink in for a minute before bursting out again: "Wait!"

"Wait, what?" Max seemed surprised at the random outburst.

"I haven't hacked up a hairball in hours."

"Good for you, Madison." He looked at her like her head was a balloon, but she didn't care. No hairballs meant good things for her.

A few hours drifted by without any reports from his friends. His worry was evident in his dark eyes, reflecting her own anxiety. Someone should have reported with information, even if there was no information to relay.

"Excuse me for a minute. I'm going to go make a few more calls to see if we can find out anything new."

Max excused himself, and Madison attempted to sit patiently, but wound up twiddling her thumbs and gnawing on her fingernails instead. Thoughts of Sarah's well being filled her with worry. She always acted inconvenienced when Sarah popped in, but she cared about her friend. She didn't want her to be harmed or die thinking she resented her.

When Max returned, he seemed slightly befuddled, confused even. "I wasn't able to get in touch with anyone. I doubt that's a good sign, and as much as I'd hate to go out there blind, I don't think we have any other option."

"So, when your friends are in trouble we go running, but when mine has obviously been taken we do nothing?" Madison clenched her fists and narrowed her eyes at Max, awaiting a reply.

"It's not like that, and you know it." Max looked her way with soft, pleading eyes. "We just don't have a choice. I didn't want to rush out this close to the full moon, but it's the only way."

She had forgotten about the moon and was suddenly uncomfortable about heading out to save Sarah and the merry men.

Madison didn't really know what would happen when she shifted; last time she'd passed out before anything interesting had happened. So, she was afraid of what would happen to her out in the open, unprotected and away from the warm embrace of Max King. "Shit, I forgot all about the full moon. Do you think

I'll be okay if we get stuck out there when the moon rises? I don't know what will happen to me."

"I'm not sure. You're new at this and that can be difficult. It's been a long time for me. I don't remember what those first times were like, but they weren't great. I will try to stay by your side at all times, but I just have no idea what's lurking out there. All of my people are missing. I can't be certain what kind of manpower we'll be up against."

"Can we even risk going out there?" She still wanted to save Sarah, but she didn't want to wind up dead or maiming strangers, even the "bad guy" kind, in the process ... which seemed like a distinct possibility in this weird new world.

Madison wished more than ever that this whole debacle had never happened, even if she had just had the most amazing sex of her life with an Adonis.

What do I do? What do I do? What do I do?

She had to make the choice between saving her only friend who may, in fact, be one of the bad people; and saving her own hide, figuratively speaking.

While her new condition wasn't without its perks, she found it harder and harder to maintain her sarcastic demeanor and classic wit. Her personality, the core of her being, was slipping away in the stress of being a newborn shifter caught in some sort of turf war. She was reduced to a flailing, fluffy, whiney thing, amazed at how ignorant she was to the rest of the world.

"Madison, are you okay?"

Max stared at her as if she were a fragile porcelain doll or perhaps, a newborn babe. "No, Max, I'm not okay, but there isn't much we can do about it, is there?"

"You've got me. I don't know how much that helps, but at least you're not alone in this." He reached out to touch her arm, a gesture of solidarity.

"Thanks, but that doesn't do much to ease my tension. While I may not be alone, I'm an inexperienced Wisconsin weirdo."

"Not weird, Madison, unique ... beautiful ... strong ... a real find."

She smiled at him. He was trying to boost morale, but it wasn't helping. Deep down, she knew who and what she was. His starry-eyed view of her didn't change the core of her being.

"What's our plan of attack?" she asked, attempting to shift the focus from herself to the matter at hand.

"We have to go back to Wisconsin. We have to go home."

13

"WE CAN'T EXACTLY charge back over the state line with no direction, can we?" Madison was a bit frustrated with their lack of an itinerary. She felt safe in Max's fancy Chicago condo and didn't want to blindly rush into danger without some kind of concrete plan. "I mean, we don't even know if they're still at their compound or whatever, right? Even if they are, they could be anywhere between Lake Geneva and Green Bay by now. Hell, they could be in Iowa. So, how are we even going to find them ... whoever they are?"

"I imagine 'they' are Mainfield and his lackeys. The 'where' is a bit trickier. You're right about that. We need to do a little more reconnaissance before we charge into the battlefront. The two of us aren't much of a cavalry as it is, so a location and plan may help."

"That's what I'm saying." She felt triumphant in her victory. Her need for structure won out. Home was a little under two hours away. So, they had some time to plan during the drive.

Max paced in the living room, scratching his chin, and looking perturbed. She knew he'd been at this for a while and that he was strong and successful, but felt he may have stretched himself too thin this time. Some of his confident veneer had melted and she worried that his stress meant bad things were coming.

"It was the best sex of my life," she blurted out.

"Wait, what did you just say?"

She smiled at him coyly. "You heard me."

"Thanks for the compliment, but that has nothing to do with ... Wait!"

"Wait?" Her attempt to lighten the mood had seemingly sparked an idea in Max.

"Cellphones," Max shouted.

"Yes, cellphones are pretty handy devices ..."

"No, Madison, that's not it. My friends all had their cellphones on them."

"So ...?"

"So ... cells have GPS locaters in them."

Not understanding the connection, she shrugged before replying. "I don't see how that helps us, unless you're some sort of rockin' techno-path."

"I'm not, but I have a friend in the police department who could run a trace on the phones for me." He smiled, pausing his pacing, standing just a bit straighter.

"Well, then why are you standing around arguing with me?" she replied. "Do it. Time is of the essence here. Our biological clocks are sort of ticking, and I'd rather not get caught out in the open when it's time to play with kitty."

Max ran off again to call his friend while Madison was left to her own devices. She didn't have any more nails to nibble. In fact, she didn't have much of anything to nibble and her stomach was growling something fierce.

She couldn't remember the last time she'd eaten and that coffee was burning a hole through her stomach lining. "Max, you got any grub in this place? A lady like myself needs to eat ... now."

"Yeah, hold on a minute, Mad. I'll fix you something to eat when I'm off the phone."

Feeling impatient, she decided to poke around in the kitchen. The man had all sorts of strange cooking implements, half of which she didn't recognize. Some cook she was—her culinary skills were limited to tailgating cuisine and the occasional mac and cheese.

The fridge was packed, but she didn't see much that she recognized. So, she moved to the cabinets. "Ah ha, Lucky Charms!"

Madison pulled out a huge mixing bowl and filled it with the entire box of cereal. She decided to brave the refrigerator once again to find some milk. After moving a few things around, she found some almond milk stuffed at the back of the fridge. She emptied its contents into her bowl.

"So, I see you couldn't wait. I would have fixed you an actual meal—"

"This is meal enough for me," she said while shoveling delicious cereal into her mouth.

He smiled, but there was something new in that smile ... something she couldn't quite identify. "You've got some milk spilling out of your mouth."

Feeling a bit mortified before quickly wiping away the milk, Madison asked, "So, what's the verdict?"

Max grinned and held up a piece of paper. "They're all somewhere in Janesville, Wisconsin. I've got the address right here. I don't know if your friend is with them, but it's the best lead we've got. Whaddaya say?"

"I say we go ... once I'm finished, of course."

"You know," he replied, "you are much braver than you let on. You're willing to put your life on the line to save someone we're not even sure needs saving. I really hope this Sarah person is the friend you want her to be."

She nodded, unsure of whether he'd given her a compliment or not, while she spooned another soggy mess into her mouth.

•　　•　　•

After Madison finished her enormous bowl of cereal, she slipped on her shoes, ready to head out into the harsh streets of Janesville, Wisconsin. Since Max had pretty much torn her clothing to shreds and the blanket dress she'd been wandering around in didn't seem suitable for public consumption, she had donned some of his clothes.

She felt uncomfortable, his shirt clinging tight to her body, the fabrics stiffer, itchier than she preferred. At least the man had sweatpants, ones that clung to her generous thighs. There would be no saving his shirt, though. The top half was stretched beyond recovery.

"At least we don't match," he chided. "We do have a long road ahead of us. I'm betting there'll be a Walmart to stop at before we reach our destination."

She relaxed a bit at the thought of a Walmart, as it was so normal. She hadn't even considered stopping at a store to purchase new clothes. Life was overwhelming her common sense a bit.

With that, they piled back into Max's car and began the journey back into the great state of Wisconsin.

14

"YOU REALIZE WE'VE ONLY GOT about sixteen hours left?" Madison mused with a mouth full of fried fast food goodness.

They had just made their Walmart visit, and she had selected some more appropriate attire, which Max paid for as her wallet was M.I.A.

"Yes, Madison, I know. Hopefully, we can get in, get everyone and get out without being detected."

"Yeah, like that's going to happen."

"Thanks for the vote of confidence."

They drove on in an uncomfortable silence. The highway was unbelievably calm, and they made it from Chicago to the Wisconsin border in record time. It would only be about an hour before they reached their destination, so long as no more freaky stuff happened.

She was pretty fed up with all of the freaky stuff. The great sex and the super hot man were acceptable, but she had enough of the rest of this bullshit.

"Are you sure this will work?" She asked.

"Well, let's start by driving past to case the joint—"

"Ha, you said 'case the joint'—"

"Madison, can we focus here?"

"Yes, Captain. Go on."

"And once we have a look at what we're up against, we can decide from there. I would imagine they've got us pretty outnumbered, but maybe we can use that to our advantage. It's much easier to sneak two shifters into a building than it is to sneak in a whole troop."

"In case you haven't noticed, I'm not exactly the sneaky type. It'll be like trying to sneak an elephant into the opera."

"Madison, I think you severely underestimate yourself."

"No, I think my assessment is pretty accurate."

"Whatever. You're an impossible woman." It seemed to her that Max was getting frustrated with all of her down-putting. "Anyway, let's just get there and drive past before we make any real decisions."

Madison and Max made their way to Janesville in the early afternoon. They had made a few more pit stops for food and supplies as they weren't sure what kind of lion's den they'd be romping into. *Thank goodness for Kwik Trips.*

Ten hours remained until the rise of the full moon. Max hoped they'd have enough time to get his kin out before the shift overtook them, but the situation was as grim as they were clueless.

"Okay, that's the building, Mad. What do you think?" The GPS tracker led them to a shoddy run-down warehouse downtown. The rusted excuse for a building had likely been condemned long ago.

"I think that place is a shit hole," she replied.

"Yes, that's obvious, but do you have any helpful observations?"

"No, remember I'm new with all of this. I wouldn't even know what to look for. I've been to Janesville before, but I haven't really explored this part of town."

He shouldn't have expected her to form the plan—he was the experienced one. "Well, I think we should wait until it gets darker before taking any action. We can park down the street and try to sneak in one of those windows, provided we can find one that isn't boarded up."

"Sure, let's do that."

Madison and Max went to a café down the street and ordered coffee as they would need all their energy to withstand the coming evening. Her hands shook holding the coffee, betraying her fear. And the lump in her throat was most definitely a hairball that the hot liquid couldn't get past. She paused for a few moments to calm herself.

It's okay. I'm okay. It's okay. I'm okay.

She felt the lump recede and her airway opened back up.

"Max, what happens if we get caught? Or, what if this is a trap? I'm scared." Madison trembled, seemingly to shrink back into herself, fear beginning to take hold.

"I know, I don't feel as confident as I'd like to, but this is all we've got. We can't go to the police—they'd most likely just laugh at us; they don't need to know about shifters just yet— and we can't wait around too long because I don't want you to get caught in a bad situation when the moon rises."

"I think we're going to be caught in a bad situation no matter what."

"You don't know that, sweetheart. Calm down. Let's just take things as they come, okay?"

Did he call me sweetheart? "I guess so, but I'd rather take you as you cum." She winked at him.

"I see, well, that could be fun."

They finished their coffee and headed back to Max's car for a little afternoon delight. Of course, they had to move the car to a more discreet location before going at it, but Max didn't put up a fight. Madison hoped he was saving that energy for something else.

While she usually preferred to have sex in the dark, while drunk, something about the man made her inhibitions fall by the wayside. She's been nearly nude in his apartment for hours and he didn't gag one time. For the first time in a long time, she left her hangups behind and threw herself into the moment. By the time they were finished with another round of mind-blowing, earth-moving sex, the sky began to darken. They dressed and hurried back toward the warehouse.

"You ready, Madison?" Max asked. He tapped his watch, subtly letting her know it was time to leave the apartment and head back to Wisconsin.

"As ready as I'll ever be. At least I can die happy, what with all of the sex."

"Thanks, I'm a stud." He flashed her his signature smile before going into business mode.

"Pshh! And I'm not?"

"No, no, you're quite adept." He smiled at her. "Madison, it's more than sex, you know that, right?"

"Isn't there something taboo about our kinds intermingling? Like isn't it frowned upon to consort with other cat species?"

"That's not how it works. Obviously, I don't want to be with a rat or anything, but there is nothing forbidding the two of us from being together indefinitely."

"Erm ..." She didn't know where the man was going with this. "Indefinitely" was a weighty word.

"Oh? That's all you have to say?" He had a pained expression scrawled across his face once again.

"Well, why don't we discuss this when all is said and done?" She was sure, from Max's expression, that he didn't know how to read her reaction.

"Okay, we can do that."

She kissed him on the cheek, not wanting to hurt his feelings. "Rain check, for sure."

She involuntarily winked again; it was contagious. This must have been why Max was always doing it.

His mood seemed to lighten a bit. "Sure, but I'm holding you to it."

"I hope that's not the only thing you'll be holding to me."

He laughed. "We've only got about five hours until the shifting overtakes us, which means we should get going. I don't want to be caught unaware. We need to be as ready as possible."

Madison reluctantly followed Max toward the decrepit building. She could smell something was off. She didn't recognize the scent, but with her feline senses, it was hard to decipher what was what. Smells overwhelmed her in a way they never had before. Some of them were intoxicating, mouth-watering and some were vile. Something acrid was permeating her senses, blanketing her field of smell. "Max, do you smell something weird?"

"A bit."

"Do you know what it is? I think it smells like dead fish. You know, the kind that's been roasting in the sunlight while sitting in the backseat of someone's car for a few days?"

"Is that a scent you're intimately familiar with?" he asked, seeming entertained and repulsed. "It's just filth, Madison. Sweat, body odor, and maybe some waste. I think it's the shifters. They must be huddled together and captive somewhere nearby."

"That's a pretty big building; how are we going to locate them?"

"Follow your nose, like Toucan Sam."

"Jokes, at a time like this, Max? Come on!"

"You clearly like cereal. I thought you'd appreciate the jab. But I'm serious. The closer we get, the stronger that smell will get."

"Okay, then." She was embarrassed for not realizing that, but she was still a newbie.

She and Max were in stealth mode—rather, as stealthy as two shifters could be. Madison wasn't exactly dainty or graceful.

As they sidled along the building, the odor grew stronger, fouler, and she had a hard time not losing her coffee and fast food all over the lawn.

"How can you bear that smell?" she whispered.

"You'll get used to it after a while."

"Gross. I hope I never have to smell something like this again."

"You're in for a rude awakening. The world is a stinky place, Madison, but we shouldn't be talking right now. I don't want to give them any more of an advantage than they already have."

She shut up for a minute but couldn't help thinking about the stench. If she could smell them, they could probably smell her as well. "Max?"

"What Madison?" He gave her an irritated scowl.

"Can they smell us, too?"

The thought had to have occurred to him, but maybe he didn't want to add any more stress to the situation than was necessary. "Technically, yes, but hopefully their stench overpowers our scents."

"Okay, then." She hadn't thought of that, so it calmed her nerves. They were almost at the windows and Madison prayed they could find one with loose boards or one that wasn't boarded at all.

Most of the building was sealed up, but some of the boards were rotted. Max signaled for Madison to stay put before he went ahead to look for an entrance.

Madison stood, feeling cold in the night air, waiting on Max's return. She was nauseated by the smell wafting straight through her nostrils. She gagged. Preoccupied by the foul scents, she's failed to notice the heavy footsteps thudding along behind her until it was too late.

She turned towards the source of the sound and found herself face-to-face with one of the thugs from her hotel room.

"Hello, Madison." The man smiled at her, his rotted teeth in full view, before reaching back and slugging her right in the head.

15

T HE MORTIFYING STENCH reeled Madison back toward consciousness this time. She must have been in the belly of the beast. The rotting stink was unbearable. She retched before her eyes even had the chance to focus. Her vomit only made the stench worse, and fried foods didn't taste so good the second time around.

She wiped her face with her sleeve and sat up. After composing herself, she peered around. She was in a large room with high ceilings. The walls were green with splotches of orange, rust, no doubt. Filth coated the concrete floor. When her eyes focused in the dim room, she noticed she was not alone.

The room was full of random people—Max's merry men (and women) she assumed, though she couldn't make out Sarah from her vantage point.

Madison also saw no sign of Max, so perhaps not all was lost. "Where am I?"

The man next to her, a feline shifter named George, was the first to respond. Madison wasn't quite sure how or why she knew this man. There were obviously some pieces missing here, but she was rather positive that George was his name and that his face was a familiar one.

"Mainfield and his goons have us all locked away in this room," George said.

Well, that cleared up the who part, but why were they being held? "Why is he keeping us locked up?" Madison asked.

George responded. "He's making a power play for the shifter world and with us out of the way, things will be a bit easier for him. He's also waiting for some tiger to join him in battle. I personally think he's full of it because there's no such thing as a tiger shifter. Tiger shifters are a thing of myth."

"They are?"

He gaped at her like she had three eyes or four arms. "You must be new?"

"Brand-spanking."

"You see, the tiger shifter is supposed to come of age and determine the fate of the shifter world. If the tiger were to team up with Mainfield we'd be toast, but since there's no such thing as a tiger shifter, I'd say we have a fighting chance."

"But we're all locked up." Madison rubbed her throbbing temple before tentatively poking her aching cheek. She wondered if he'd broken a bone in her face or if she'd just wind up with some nasty bruises. Hoping her new shifter powers extended to accelerated heating, she shook off her grogginess as best she could.

"Yeah, but in a few hours the change will happen, and we'll be able to get out of this room. It's just getting past Mainfield's kitties that worries me. At least we'll have a fighting chance."

"Great. I've never shifted during the moon before. This is gonna be awful."

"Then, you're not going to be of any use to us. We're hoping that some of our friends catch wind of our captivity and come to join the fray, but you should probably go over there in the corner with the other newbie and stay out of the way."

Other newbie? Madison felt a little bit less alone knowing she wasn't the only new shifter in the pack. She was about to make her way in the direction George had gestured, but she hesitated to ask him one last question. "So, you guys can't just shift now and get out of here?"

"A few of us can, but many of the shifters in here are wolves. So, it's best to wait for the moon and all shift together."

"I see ..." She was stuck in a room full of werewolves. This was not a situation she'd ever imagined. Part of her wanted to laugh. The rest of her was petrified.

For Madison Murphy, the excitement was non-stop. She caught a glimpse of the small figure huddled in the corner.

Sarah! "Sarah! Sarah, Sarah, Sarah!"

The small figure blinked up at her, a glimpse of hope in her swollen eyes. "Madison, is that you?" she squeaked.

"Oh, Sarah, I've never been happier to see you in my life, no offense, it is nice to see you most of the time, but I am so relieved you're okay." Madison was also relieved that Sarah wasn't one of the bad guys, but she didn't want to let Sarah in on that one. She felt bad enough for distrusting her friend in the first place. "What's going on here?"

"I don't know. I woke up in the trunk of a car, and I was all tied up. When we got here, they just tossed me in with all of these people ... shifters, I guess? I don't know anymore. They've sort of ostracized me because I had no idea what was happening."

"It's okay. I'm here now." Madison said, grabbing her friend and hugging her close, "We can be ostracized together. So, I guess you know you get to be a shifter, too, huh?"

"Yeah, I sort of figured that one out when they tossed me in here with this bite mark on my wrist. I should have listened to you and stayed home ... I just wanted a little bit of excitement in my life. This is much more than I bargained for."

"It's okay, Sarah, we'll just have to sit tight. Max is out there somewhere; there's still hope that we'll make it out of here before shifting."

"Madison, the moon is going to be up in less than an hour. I don't think Max can dispatch all of the bad guys and break us out in time."

"Well, at least we won't have to shift alone. We can do it with all of these folks and follow them out into battle. There's power in numbers."

Sarah looked slightly less forlorn, but tears dripped down her cheeks. "But I don't know how to fight. I cry when I chip my nail polish; this isn't going to work out for me."

"Hopefully, your animal can fight, then. If not, stay behind me. Okay?"

"Okay." Sarah nodded.

"Let me take care of you for once. Everyone keeps saying I'm a big deal. Maybe they're right. I'll do my best to protect you when the time comes."

Sarah was scared, but Madison couldn't blame her. She would have been petrified if she were in Sarah's position. Not that she wasn't also scared. "Do you know what sort of animal you are?"

"No."

"Well, has your hearing or sight or smell improved since you got turned?"

"No. I don't think so."

"Then you're probably not a cat. That sort of thing happens to cats. I guess we'll just find out when the moon rises."

"Yippee," Sarah chimed with false excitement.

"Maybe it'll be cool. You could be a dragon! Or, maybe you're a giant eagle and you can fly right out of here! That would be good, right?"

Sarah nodded, seeming unconvinced. Madison grabbed her hand and squeezed it, "We are on a great adventure, right?"

Sarah nodded again.

"Then, let's try to kick some ass, okay?"

16

T HE MINUTES WOUND DOWN, and there was still no sign of Max. Mainfield's men filtered into the room and gathered in front of the door. It was intended as a barricade to ensure the prisoners wouldn't escape when the change came, but Madison knew better. There was going to be a big, gross bloody battle no matter what. These thugs were twitchy, cracking their necks and knuckles, gearing up for a brawl.

She imagined the other "good guy" shifters were ready for battle, but Mainfield still obviously felt like he had the upper hand. She wasn't sure why, since she was locked up with everyone else, but something didn't sit right with her. *What is he up to?*

One of the goons opened the door. She thought it was Frank but couldn't be sure at this distance. They weren't very familiar with one another having only met in passing. The maybe Frank made his way through the crowd and grabbed her by the collar, dragging her out with him.

"No, let her go," Sarah cried.

The man slapped her in the face, and she recoiled, curling up in the corner again.

"It's okay, Sarah. I will be fine. Stay here with the good guys."

The Frank-man harshly pulled her through the door, slamming it behind him, and tossing her at the feet of someone wearing expensive Italian loafers before anyone could react or come to her aid. She was willing to bet those shoes belonged to Arthur.

"Hello, Ms. Murphy, it's so good to see you again. I hope you've been enjoying our hospitality."

She spat on his shoes before looking up at him to respond. "Yes, I've found the accommodations quite suitable, and if you don't mind, I'll be going back now."

She was worried about Sarah and wanted to be with the other shifters when things started happening. Madison's palms began to sweat, and her heart seemed to beat just a tad bit faster than usual. A burning sensation filled her eyes, and despite her rubbing them, she couldn't quell the pain. It was like she'd been swimming around in chlorine all day, a sensation that didn't make sense, but one she shrugged off as part of her forced shifting.

Everything seemed brighter, clearer. A strange tingling under her skin told her the full moon was close, fifteen minutes maybe.

"Um, I don't think that's going to happen. I have another proposal for you, and I think you won't be able to resist this one. You were lucky last time, but even if your little lion friend is around here somewhere, I don't think he'll get past my men in time to save you." Arthur puffed his chest out, seeming cocky, like he had everything figured out, the conclusion of this whole ordeal was set in stone.

Madison met his gaze, unwilling to yield to another bully. She'd faced so many during her lifetime and she was tired of it. "Yeah. So? I don't see why that's going to stop me from saying no to you and your stupid proposal."

"But, you see, I'm offering you a once in a lifetime opportunity. I really mean that ... no one will ever present you with anything close to it."

"How do you know?" she responded, trying to maintain a cocky and self-assured attitude.

"Because, Ms. Murphy, if you refuse, I am going to kill you, and there's not much you can do about that."

"Yikes, well that does pose a problem, doesn't it?"

"Only for you, Madison, only for you. I'm okay with the outcome either way." He was lying. She was certain of that.

Now that she knew the truth about the tiger shifter, Mainfield couldn't afford to lose her. He knew she was valuable, but he didn't know she knew it too. She needed to play that card right. So, she puffed out her ample chest and responded in kind, mirroring his confidence. "And if you kill me, who'll tip the balance of the scales in your favor? How will you get control of the shifters?"

He blinked at her response. "If you do not join us, I cannot afford to let you live, lest you tip the scales the other way. So, you see, it would be in my best interest to kill you."

She hadn't thought of that; sweat beaded and rolled down her back. She couldn't deceive the man, he would catch her lie, but she also wasn't willing to join him.

"So, Madison, what do you say?"

She attempted to appear as if she was actually considering his proposal, hoping she could stall for time.

"Answer me now or die. It's as simple as that."

Madison glanced down briefly. She raised her head, and with a confidence she didn't know she had, said, "Go to hell, you asshole. I'd rather die."

Mainfield's expression dripped with disappointment as he pulled a gun from his waistband. He had it aimed at her head, safety clicked off. "That was a poor decision, Madison. It's such a shame to have to kill you."

"You don't have it in you," she spat before squeezing her eyes shut, not wanting to watch the last few seconds of her life. However, before he could pull the trigger, the gun clattered to the ground. They both doubled over in pain. The change was upon them.

17

MADISON HEARD THE CAPTIVES screeching out in pain before crying out herself. She knew shifting was a painful process, but she wasn't prepared for the immense burning sensation coupled with the breaking of her bones.

After dropping to the ground, she curled into the fetal position while clutching her roiling stomach. Her insides throbbed as the beast within attempted to find release. Each of her nerves felt as if they were being seared by a red-hot poker, and her panicked breaths sent stabbing pains to her irate stomach. She could feel hot blood rushing through her veins to fuel the tedious shifting process.

Her skin actually began to shred, sloughing off her body, and making way for the fur that began to sprout. "What the fuck?" she screamed as large flaps of skin fell to the ground beneath her. She tried not to freak out, but while watching her skin tear off in sheets and tumble to the ground, she lost control, terror overcoming her, as she witnessed something that would have been more at home in a horror movie than in real life.

As she attempted to slow her racing heart by taking deep slow breaths, the convulsions started. She imagined they were similar to the contractions a woman felt during childbirth, except these ran through her entire body.

Searing pain ripped through her as she writhed on the ground. Bright white fur sprouted in waves across her now bulging muscles. The black stripes would fill in the blanks later, but she wasn't able to focus long enough to witness that particular spectacle.

"Oww!" she screeched as her spine rearranged itself—vertebrae crunching and stretching all at once. It felt as if her remaining bones had been torn out through her skin to make room for something new. The bones in her arms and legs twisted and contorted before snapping and reforming into strong legs and paws. With each snap, a horrid new convulsion raged through her misshapen form. She tried to scream out again but heard only the howls of an animal in terrible pain.

Her vocal cords must have been lost somewhere during the transformation. By the time her face began to elongate and reshape itself, Madison was numb from the pain. She gave herself over to the process.

The next memory she had was that of her tail flailing wildly. Strangely, she still felt very human on the inside. Her mind thought in human words even though roars came from her newly-found mouth. While she had survived the actual shifting process, the prospect of facing an army of rabid enemies still daunted her.

Drained from being completely rearranged, Madison took a moment to admire her new shape. She stood an impressive two feet taller than your run-of-the-mill tiger. She was also a bit wider, which was to be expected considering her chubby human form.

In her confusion, she had lost track of Arthur. It was probably not a great twist to her day, but this was her first full moon shifting experience, and it was rather overwhelming.

Arthur was afraid of her tiger form. He could have easily bested her human form by pulling that trigger, but now the playing field may be leveled. Madison turned and trotted towards the room from which she had been pulled. She jumped up, using her paws to press at the door. But nothing happened. She couldn't budge it with her weight alone, a fact she found entertaining.

She paced back and forth, impatiently, trying to figure out how to get into the room with the rest of the shifters. She could hear their cries and wanted to join the fray. She wanted to keep good on her promise to protect Sarah as well.

She backed up as far as she could, away from the door, and squared up with it. Madison put her head down and ran full force at the door, using her hard head to bust right through it. The door splintered under the force of her collision and she bounded her way into the battle.

Uncertain how to communicate with her brethren, she gave a great roar, which momentarily halted the fray.

The room full of four-legged creatures stopped to gape at her. She didn't know who was who, but she was able to spot the good guys in the crowd. There was something faintly human about their eyes, a light of some sort. The other shifters had cold, hard eyes all of which were pointed in her direction.

Most of the shifters had finished their transformation, and the few stragglers were close to completion. Some had already begun snapping at one another. Madison could smell a hint of rust-scented blood in the air.

The battle was at a standstill because the prodigal tiger shifter had finally appeared. Max and Arthur had been telling the truth, she truly was a big deal. Madison took a quick look around to access her surroundings, as the fight wouldn't stay paused forever.

There were wolves, hyenas, a few monkeys, cougars, jaguars, hawks and bears littering the floor of the abandoned warehouse. There was also an estranged ostrich huddled up in a far corner of the building.

And, of course, there was still no sign of Max. *That asshole better not stand me up this time, and if he's dead I'm going to kill him ... again!*

Madison heard a roar from behind her. She turned to face a great lion. Unfortunately, it wasn't Max. She could tell by the cold dead eyes that she was looking directly at Arthur Mainfield. He was gunning for her—teeth barred and claws ready as he charged in her direction.

The world slowed down as Arthur made his approach. Madison could see the other shifters leaping into battle. There were claws, tearing flesh and fur flying in all directions.

She had no idea who had the upper hand, but she did know she was in deep trouble. The foul heart beating within Arthur Mainfield's chest had one agenda, to kill her.

Several shifters charged the lion from each side, slowing down his progress. She assumed it was a strategic move, that dispatching the head honcho would give them a swift win.

Mainfield, however, was not to be underestimated. He roared, his huge golden body shaking as he raised his claws in the air. He tore out their throats mercilessly.

Madison was petrified, unmoving. Fallen shifters now lay splayed across the ground, littered in lifeless clumps. Hope waning, but not lost, Madison charged forward to join the fray. She lashed out and dispatched a few of Mainfield's men, though she didn't kill them. She couldn't bring herself to take a life. Blood splattered across the dilapidated walls; it pooled on the floor.

Madison had no quick escape. Even the scared ostrich had joined the violent fray as it was also out of options. It ran head bowed down and head-butted anything in its path. Ostriches turned out to be surprisingly useful in battle; it dispatched at least five shifters in the short time Madison was able to pay attention.

She squared her feline shoulders as Mainfield recovered from his early efforts and swiftly closed in on her. The man had promised to kill her, and it was obvious that it was number one on his to do list. His eyes were full of hatred, and he wanted blood ... *her* blood.

So, she stood her ground, braced and ready for the killing blow. The magnificent tiger struck down in its first battle. She hoped that wasn't her fate, but she had a terrible feeling she was about to become a martyr.

Blood dripped down Arthur's bulging muscles, matting his illustrious mane.

Tears stung Madison's eyes, and her throat burned as she let out one final roar. She'd fight him with her teeth and claws, even if it meant losing to his seasoned shifter form. Just as he was about to strike, something large and fast leaped in their direction and the two creatures tumbled away in a big yellow blur.

Blinking twice, Madison realized it was another lion. *Max!*

He had come to her rescue. Again. The man had a knack for timing. She thought he might just be worth keeping, but she didn't let her head drift too far because a large, bloody battle was still being waged.

The smaller lion pinned Mainfield to the floor. The other animals had stopped fighting to turn their attention to the two lions. Some howled in solidarity and others growled at the prospect of more blood. The smaller lion gave a great roar, and in one fell swoop tore out Arthur's throat. Arthur went limp as blood pooled around his fallen form.

The other animals just stared wide-eyed in amazement. Everything was at a standstill. No one had expected the quick dispatch of the big bad and they didn't know what to do. By the end of the fray, the peak of the full moon had already begun to wane.

Madison could feel what was left of energy quickly draining from her body as she collapsed in exhaustion. The smaller lion slowly padded its way toward her crumpled form as she looked up at it with grateful eyes.

Max gently nudged her with his proud nose before collapsing next to her and laying his head on her chest. In her final waking moments, Madison watched the shifters fall to the ground in exhaustion as the moon slipped back behind the horizon.

18

WHEN MADISON AWOKE, she was naked and covered in scrapes and dried blood. She had a hard time keeping her eyes open, but she did notice a naked form cradled next to her. Max ... he had come to save her. She remembered thinking her life was forfeit as he charged in to save the day. Again.

She could get used to waking up next to him; of course, she would prefer it if they didn't have to be covered in blood and guts each time, but she was also willing to compromise. She'd pay almost any price to keep waking up next to the man who had saved her life, more than once.

Noticing her nudity, Madison was mortified that a room full of people would see her generous body. There were no clothes. There was very little she could use to cover herself with.

Max stirred, rubbing his eyes. "Did we win?" he asked, his voice slurred with sleep.

"How should I know? I don't even know which ones are the good guys anymore. Everyone's just laying around naked."

"Well, Mainfield is dead, right?" he asked.

"You did tear his throat out, Max. People don't recover from those sorts of injuries." She used an arm to cover her breasts and another the shield her pubic region.

"Stop that." Max said, "You don't need to cover up. Everyone's naked. It's fine."

The other naked bodies began to move and slowly, the survivors sat up to stretch. However, a good deal of the bodies never moved. At least half of the shifters hadn't survived the evening.

Mainfield's men littered the ground, but many of Max's friends were also deceased. With Mainfield dead, his men had no leader and were not an immediate threat.

The bad shifters awoke, scrambled to get up, then hastily left the room. There was no need for more carnage. So, cautiously watching, Max's men let them leave.

Once alone, the good guys began collecting the bodies of their fallen brethren, tossing them over their shoulders, ready to haul them away in order to give them a proper burial.

Max rose to solemnly address his band of merry men, nodding at them in solidarity as they ushered themselves out the door. They scuttled out into the world, hoping to get somewhere safe before too many humans awoke to a troop of nude bloodied people with dead bodies over their shoulders running through town.

Snapping back to reality, Madison remembered her scared friend. "Sarah, where's Sarah?"

There was no sign of the small blonde woman. "I don't know, Madison. She may not have made it."

"She has to have made it. I don't know what I would do if she didn't."

The remaining shifters, Max, and Madison searched long and hard for Madison's blonde cohort, but to no avail. As they were about to give up their search, they heard muffled cries.

Max and Madison closed in on the source of the noise, but they didn't see much of anything. Still, something was alive somewhere in the cesspool.

After scanning the ground, Madison noticed a few fingers barely waggling. Someone was trapped beneath the fallen bodies of a few dead shifters. *How gross.*

Max went to work uncovering the mysterious person. When he finally freed the unfortunate captive, he helped her sit up. It was a filthy, matted, and disgruntled Sarah.

Madison rushed over to hug her friend. "Sarah! Thank God, you made it."

"I should have stayed home. That was horrible. I'm naked and covered in blood and gore."

"I told you to stay home, didn't I?"

"You should have made me mind my own business!" Sarah screeched.

"As if my telling you to stay at home would have made a difference. You're way too nosy to not go poking around in dangerous affairs."

"I am not."

"Of course, not ..." Madison, not keen on her breast swinging in her friend's face, went to the corner of the room where a stack of empty cardboard boxes sat. She retrieved three and brought them back so everyone could cover their private parts.

"So, which animal were you?" Madison asked, more comfortable with conversation now that she was wearing a fashionable box.

"Guess."

"I have no idea. It was a zoo in here. There was even an ostrich running around and headbutting things. This is all too much for me."

At that, Max chimed in, "There was an ostrich? That's weird, I've never seen one of those before."

Sarah raised her hand. "Yeah, that's me. The were-ostrich."

"Of course you're an ostrich. Why wouldn't you be." Madison responded. Although amused that Sarah was a shapeshifting ostrich, Madison was just happy to see that they had survived the night.

"This is Max, by the way." Madison gestured toward Max's mostly nude form.

"Nice to meet you and all that jazz, but can we just go home?"

This was the first time Madison had ever known Sarah to be antisocial, especially in the presence of an attractive male. Madison thought Sarah would be the first one to appreciate Max's assets, which were prominently displayed at the moment. "Sure, Sarah, let's do that."

They made their way toward Max's car. Madison was thankful that the small city was still sleeping and that she'd had the idea to wear boxes. She didn't think she'd be able to traipse around naked in front of other people, not today, not ever.

They piled into Max's car. He slipped into the clothes Madison had discarded after her Walmart trip as the girls remained in their fashionable boxes.

He drove the short way back to their homes and dropped them off in front of the apartment building. They looked worse for wear, but the city had probably seen stranger things.

"So, I guess I'll be seeing you ladies," he offered.

"I guess so," Sarah said before making a break for the building.

Madison stayed behind to give him an appropriate send off. "Thanks for the ride ... and all the other stuff ... saving my life and all ..."

"You're welcome. You'd better get inside before people start waking up."

She was a little disappointed with his response, but she decided to hustle and get inside before anyone else had to see her naked. "Okay."

"I'll see ya around, toots."

"Did you just call me 'toots'? That's ridiculous."

"As if the rest of the night wasn't ridiculous."

Her shoulders slumped a little in defeat at his comment, but she remained silent.

"Fine, Madison, go home."

"Fine."

"Goodbye."

"Yeah, goodbye, Max." With that, she turned, and walked into her apartment building. She begrudgingly made her way to her home, cleaned up as best she could and then collapsed in an exhausted lump on her own bed.

19

A MONTH LATER, Max sat on the couch in Madison's living room, the exact same couch Harold had been sitting on when he delivered the life-altering news that she was now a shifter.

She needed a new couch. This one was full of bad memories.

But Max was here now, all suave and sexy, and that certainly helped. Perhaps there was hope for the couch yet.

"So, what are you doing here?" she demanded. She watched him for a moment, looking for some sort of reaction in his face, a twitch, anything that would give away how he felt.

"You have every right to be angry, Madison, I should have at least called. I realize that now. I'm just not used to … this."

"Yeah, should have, could have, didn't. It's been a month and you didn't even bother sending me a 'Dear John' letter—nothing. What did you expect to find when you came over? Welcoming arms and a warm embrace? It's far too late for that." Lying, even to herself, she wasn't willing to roll over just because the man finally showed up. The library had given her a work-from-home job doing archival of old newspapers. She could sustain herself just fine.

"I came here to apologize, and if you don't want to hear it, that's fine."

Max seemed sincere, but being the suspicious type, she didn't trust it.

"Apologize for what ... lying to me? Abandoning me? Using me for sex? There are so many things to choose from that I just don't know what you're here to apologize for."

Hoping they could move past this ordeal and mend fences, even just in a friendly way, she should have been nicer, should have been more open to discussion, less confrontational, especially if she wanted an afternoon romp to be on the table.

"No Madison, everything I said was the truth, and while I did enjoy the sex, it wasn't the only reason I wanted to be with you. You're an amazing, witty, and beautiful woman."

"Spare me. I don't need to listen to more of your crap."

"I mean it. You're pretty swell."

"Swell? Great word. Of course, I'm swell, but that doesn't mean someone like you would appreciate my ample good qualities."

"Someone like me? What does that even mean? Seriously, I'm trying to apologize. Can you just hear me out? I'll say my piece, then go if that's what needs to happen, though I hope you'll reconsider me."

He winked. "I should have come in with you the morning after the big bad battle, I know that. But I needed some time to process the gravity of the situation and the weight of my feelings."

"Like the rest of us didn't have anything to process? That night was a confusing whirlwind of a bloodbath. I've never even seen a dead body in real life before. Now I've seen a whole heap of them." Madison was boiling, thankfully she'd grown accustomed to suppressing her shifting abilities.

She had become a shifter, gotten kidnapped more than once, and almost died a handful of times in just a few short weeks and *he* had to process. That was pure golden crap.

"That's not what I meant. I mean, of course, the results of the battle weighed heavily on me. I lost some good friends in that skirmish, and I spent some time making sure they were shown the respect they deserved. The rest of us needed to mourn and mend and move forward. But the deaths weren't my main concern—you were."

"What do you mean, I was your main concern? If I was your main concern, then why haven't I heard from you in a month?"

"I've been keeping tabs on you, making sure you were safe."

"Gross. Peeping Tom, find someone else to spy on."

"You're just being unreasonable now. Listen to me, please."

"Fine." She did sort of want to hear what he had to say, but she didn't want to make it easy.

Standing her ground had always been one of her best and worst qualities. She wasn't sure how it was serving her right now, but begrudgingly she relaxed and shut her mouth to let him continue.

"You, Madison Murphy, took me by surprise. I've never been so utterly vexed by and attracted to someone before."

"What ...?"

"Madison, shut up. I mean I've never met such an abrasive yet compassionate woman. You're my match—both in conversation and in the bedroom. I had to take some time to sort out my feelings for you and to make sure this was authentic instead of me getting swept up in pheromones and action. That's not to say that you aren't wonderful, but that I needed to trust myself again.

"The whole process should have been over in a matter of days, but it has taken me a month to figure out that the aching in the pit of my belly wasn't going to go away. My love for you, my need for you, is real. Extremely real. So, whether you like it or not, I love you, and if you don't return the sentiment, that's fine.

"I just had to come here and tell you because I couldn't go on not knowing your thoughts. I've been hoping you'd return my feelings, but I was afraid to ask."

Madison had stopped listening at "love" and honed in on it for her reply, "You *what* me? How can you even say that?

You barely know me." She was astonished. She didn't know what she had expected from him, but a declaration of love wasn't it. He was bold, beautiful and a marvelous lover—but those were all things she'd given up on a long time ago.

He continued, "Yes, I know what I like and want in a partner, and you're it. It hit me, almost immediately, though I tried to push it all aside, and I didn't want to lead you on before I had come to terms with myself. It wouldn't have been fair to you, though none of this has been particularly fair to you. I love you, Madison and we've got a long time to figure out what that means. I'm already 120 years old, and that's young for our kind, so take your time, if that's what you need."

Madison was still pissed about Max's disappearance. Who wouldn't be?

The deep need for his companionship had cast a shadow over her life as well. She'd grown physically and emotionally attached during the time they'd spent together on two long car rides, running and fighting for their lives. That sort of thing bonds people. Even though it wasn't a picture-perfect run, something had transgressed between the two of them.

Was she angry? Yes. Annoyed by the way he handled the situation? Also, yes. But, none of that outweighed what she knew in her heart was love.

Despite her individuality and the trouble she had with expressing emotion, she ultimately didn't want to risk losing the man of her dreams. Swallowing her pride was difficult, but it was worth it this one time. She didn't want to end up an old spinster, hardened by time and stuck with the bad habit of hacking up hairballs. Passing on a man who seemed everything she'd ever wanted would be foolish.

Tentatively, almost in a whisper, she replied. "I, uh ... you, too."

"What was that Madison?" He grinned.

"I love you, too, okay?"

He shrugged, turning his head away from her. *What the fuck?* Madison wasn't about to let him get away with that. Grabbing him by the back of the neck, and jerking him toward her, she forced him to meet her gaze, eye to eye. "Max, did you hear me?"

"I might have." He devilishly beamed at her like the big stupid jerk he was.

He didn't exactly meet her eyes, at first, gaze darting around in every direction but hers. She waited.

"You're an infuriating woman," he whispered, just before turning swiftly, grabbing her around the back, then pulling her in for a mind-numbing kiss, the kind that made her toes crinkle and her brain go blank for just a second.

It was several minutes before she was able to drag her satisfied mouth away from his.

"I'm sorry for staying away for so long. Do you forgive me?"

"I do, Max. I probably already had when you walked in the door. I just wanted you to work for it." She was pushing his buttons, partially for retribution and partially for amusement.

He studied her a moment longer before pulling her in for one more rough, passionate kiss.

Madison wrenched herself away, resisting his magnetic draw. "So?"

"So, what?" He asked, confused.

"What about Sarah?"

"Ugh ... why does it always have to be about Sarah? Didn't we save her? Is now really the time to talk about your friend, Madison?"

"Well, she spent most of her free time trying to hook me up, and I think I should return the favor."

"This? This is what you want to talk about immediately after I've declared my undying love for you?"

"Undying, eh? I thought it was just the regular kind."

"Undying. Eternal. Everlasting. Forever." He stood up and took her hand, drawing her towards him so their eyes could meet.

He looked her up and down before the corner of his mouth twitched up into a devious half-smile. "I don't know, Madison, this might be a dangerous adventure. I've never even met a shapeshifting ostrich before."

"What, you don't like a challenge? I'm game if you are."

He kissed her on the hand. "A challenge? I'd say I love a challenge." Eyeing her suspiciously he continued, "Let's just take this project one step at a time, okay?"

Madison giggled as she led Max toward her bedroom where she planned to keep him until she was good and exhausted.

Later, Madison Murphy leaned out the window of Max's fancy new electric car. She was a Wisconsin girl at heart, but where that once meant small-town life with cute trinket shops and spending the weekend lounging on a boat, guzzling alcoholic beverages with her friends, those things weren't for her anymore.

She loved farmer's markets, artisan cheese, cheap beer, and Midwestern sports. It was how she was bred—hearty Wisconsin stock—but they were no longer her life. She left her library job behind and had been living off her savings for the last month. She knew her life needed something different.

She was now an official member of the Wisconsin Weirdos. Magic and adventure and danger awaited. She knew shifters had day jobs and she'd find hers eventually, maybe some work-from-home tutoring situation. But there was no going back. She wouldn't want to, even if she had the chance. Her life had been stilted before Harold bit her.

Madison dressed before following her fancy boyfriend out into the night.

"Let's go slay us some bad guys." she said, looking adoringly at Max as they drove on into the night. "I think I want to be a vigilante. Can we do that? Can we fight crime together?"

He laughed, considering her question for a moment, "Slow down there, cowboy. There's plenty of time for justice."

ACKNOWLEDGMENTS

L ET'S TALK ABOUT MADISON MURPHY. When I was in graduate school in the late aughts I saw a contest for a paranormal romance novel. It ended in six days. At the time I was devouring the likes of Charlaine Harris, Kim Harrison, Karen Chance, and Vicki Pettersson and I thought to myself, I can probably do that. So, I wrote the novel in six days. It is the first longer fiction I'd ever written. It might be the first substantial fiction of any kind that I've ever written. I was in grad school for creative non-fiction and poetry.

After this book saw the light of day, I spent years writing only poetry because it was my thing or so I thought. Without writing this book, I never would have gone on to write its sister novel (my longest to date) and my three horror novellas. I never would have given fiction a fair shot, because I just didn't think I was very good at it.

As it turns out, I was wrong. Thank you to Cupid's Arrow for Publishing taking a chance on my little novella about a blind date gone wrong where the main character annoyingly hacks up hairballs and complains about her life for thirty thousand-ish words. I poured many facets of myself into the character and, love her or hate her, she is a snapshot of my neurodiverse existence in my early twenties. Though, she's much cooler than I will ever be.

Thank you to Janelle Michie for offering your perspective on my story, pushing me to make it better, and helping me curb my appetite for ellipses.

Thank you to my writing buddy F. Malanoche for always being willing to read my work and offer honest criticism or point out where I've missed an opportunity to add in a joke.

Thank you to my friends who buy my books even if they're not your thing. Your support does, has, and always will mean the world to me.

To anyone out there with an appetite for creativity, don't squelch it.

Write On!

Jessica Gleason

ABOUT THE AUTHOR

JESSICA GLEASON is a lover of horror and fantasy in their various shapes and forms and can usually be found penning gory tales deep into the night. She enjoys painting monsters with acrylics and singing a mean hair metal karaoke. Her daytime persona teaches college English and Communications in the American Midwest.

Her other releases include *Playing Hooky* (Unnerving Books), and *The Dangerous Miss Ventriloquist* and *The Fabulous Miss Fortune* (Evil Cookie Publishing).

For information on her projects, follow her on Instagram (*@j.g.writes*), where she hosts a monthly horror writer challenge, #WeWriteHorror and her website, *jgwrites.carrd.co*.